The Other Side of Me

by Jamie Gray

ABOUT THE AUTHOR

Jamie Gray has worked in the theatre industry for over twenty years and was engaged in many different roles from stage hand to stage manager (and pretty much everything else in between) He's even dared to try his hand at acting occasionally and considers himself a half decent performer, however most of his friends think he's just spent far too much time in the dark.
This is his first novel which has been somewhat influenced by (but not based on) the magical moments he's experienced.

ISBN-13: 978-1548753474
ISBN-10: 1548753475

Copyright © Jamie Gray 2017

Jamie Gray has asserted his right under the Copyrights, Designs and Patents Act 1988 to be the author of this work.

All rights reserved. No part of this publication may be reproduced, stored in a retrieval system or transmitted, in any form or by any means, without the prior written permission of the author, nor be circulated in any other form of binding or cover other than that in which it is published and without a similar condition being imposed on the purchaser.

This is a work of fiction. Names, places and characters are a product of the author's imagination and any resemblance to actual persons, living or dead, is entirely coincidental and unintended.

The Other Side of Me

by
Jamie Gray

a heart-warming tale of laughter
love & a worry monkey

For my wonderful family
☺

The Other Side of Me

Dreams hide in the shadows
Yet unspoken through fear,
As I dare not reveal them
Just in case she won't hear.
So afraid of rejection and the pain of before,
Here concealed by the darkness
Will love pass by my door?

And then she looks at me
The darkness disappears, I long to be
That special someone that she hopes to see,
And I pray she'll free the other side.
I know if she were mine
Forever in my heart a light will shine
To show the way, tomorrow we'd define
If she opens up the other side of me.

But how do I tell her and just what should I say?
She may not feel the same as I do.
Then she'll think that I'm foolish,
It may push her away,
Then my pitiful life would be through.

But then she smiles my way
With eyes so full of love that I must stay
To be with her for more than just this day,
I just have to be the other side of me.

And when you look at me
I hope you see the one you'll love, and we
Will always be together endlessly,
And there can be another side.
Please say you'll be right here
To hold my hand and chase away this fear.
My every dream becoming crystal clear,
As you open up the other side.
I know that there's another side.
Please God she frees the other side of me.

One

December 1994

Monday 19th 5.55pm - It was bitterly cold and raining heavily as Freddie Hobbs splashed along the street from college and into the Husky Dog, a lively pub in the centre of town.

He quickly took off his sopping wet coat and stamped his old leaky trainers on the mat, screwing up his toes in an effort to wring as much of the freezing cold water out of his sodden socks as possible. Then dodging around the closely packed puddles of tables and stools, which were occupied by the usual collection of strangely pungent individuals, he headed for the bar.

The Husky Dog, known locally as just the Dog, was the newest and coincidentally the cheapest drinking establishment in Swelford. This meant it was also the most popular, and as John the manager rarely took any notice of how old his customers were, the local 'cash strapped' college students made up the vast majority of his clientele and contributed most generously to his profits.

For Freddie this illicit smoke filled den of grown up aspirations had been the 'place to be' ever since the day he'd enrolled at the college when he was just sixteen. Now, just a little over a year later, he's quite the regular and by the time he'd reached the bar John already had a beer waiting for him.

"I reckon that puddle outside the front door is deep enough for fish," Freddie said, shaking the rainwater from his rat-tailed hair and drenching John's well polished counter.

"I'll make some calls then Freddie, see if anyone has any going cheap."

John reached for a handful of paper towels and started mopping up the mess.

"So where's the best looking girl in Swelford tonight?" he added as his young customer rummaged through his pockets to find some money.

"Who's that then?"

Freddie knew exactly who John meant.

"Oh come on Freddie, the pretty one who spends most days super glued to your arm."

"Oh her," Freddie said trying to sound indifferent. "Lisa's out with her boyfriend Andy, but not for long I reckon. She'll be in shortly." He slapped a handful of change on the bar and flicked out £1.25 in five and ten pence pieces.

"I don't understand you two," John said collecting the money and counting it twice. "You're always together and yet you're not 'together'. As I see it, things need to change."

"Things are the way they are, and that's good for both of us."

"Yet she never appears to be as happy with the other lads as she does when she's with you, Freddie. That's a bit of a clue if I'm not very much mistaken."

"A clue to what?"

"You know exactly what I mean."

"Just good friends mate, nothing more."

"I see everything in my bar young Freddie," John said with an exaggerated wink as he shuffled off to serve another punter. "You all think I'm a bit daft but one day you'll realise that there's nothing I don't notice around here."

"You're not daft," Freddie called after him. He picked up his pint and took a sip, "You're completely barking mad."

He turned to scan the room, only to realise that in his enthusiasm to see his best friend he was over an hour early. Lisa had said about seven and would probably be late anyway, she usually was.

So he carried his drink through the lingering haze of countless student roll-ups to an empty table, as far away as possible from the sweet herby smell that was emanating from a group of lads over by the toilets.

By the time they were eighteen most of Freddie's friends were having sex, but so far he hadn't had the pleasure. He was certainly very popular with the girls and they often clamoured to compete for his attention, which of course he loved, but none of them had ever shown any genuine interest in wanting to be his girlfriend.

In many respects Freddie wasn't overly bothered, mainly because he was too busy trying to concentrate on his exams as good grades are essential for his future plans. So he considered that working hard was best, telling himself often that he didn't have time to get bogged down in any random meaningless relationships, although he often considered a share of a little random meaningless sex would be nice.

Then there's Lisa...the lovely Lisa.

None of the girls he knew were anything like her, and he'd always believe that being her best friend was way better than being a boyfriend to any of the others, and maybe the girls knew that.

Their first encounter had been when the drama teacher at secondary school had cast them in the end of term play and then put them together as dance partners. They were both fifteen and had instantly become really good friends.

For Lisa, Freddie was the first boy who'd shown a genuine interest in her without all the attempted groping and hormonal bullshit that normally accompanied the teenage lads who hung around her.

For Freddie, Lisa was his first proper crush. He definitely still had all the hormonal bullshit, but was smart enough to realise everything was best kept under control, especially the instinctive desire to grope every inch of her developing curves.

But there was so much more to his infatuation than just a physical attraction.

He loved everything about Lisa, her fierce determination and her sense of humour, but he was particularly enamoured by the cute crinkle that appeared in the corner of her eyes every time she'd smiled in his direction.

But the best thing, never to be forgotten, had been dancing with her in that school play. With his hands barely touching her narrow waist he'd trembled as he felt the incredible warmth of her soft skin through the thin material of her costume, a moment of pure ecstasy. Just holding her hand had made his heart pound and he'd begged the hours to disappear between rehearsals because the only solution to his agony was to be with her.

Freddie had been instantly smitten and was hopelessly 'in love', but his feelings have never been spoken.

Now they're always together, almost inseparable at times, but still just as good friends and nothing more. Although Freddie often wishes it could be something else, he's really happy that she chooses to spend time with him, and isn't prepared to gamble what they have for the mere chance of a fumble in her knickers.

Like Freddie, Lisa works hard at her studies and knows exactly what she wants from life, with specific plans for a future in journalism. She's a pretty petite blonde who is extremely well organised and totally obsessive about style and fashion.

But just lately, and totally out of character, she'd been fixated on dating a 'Bad Boy', someone a little rough and unrefined, a challenge for this independent young woman to tame. She's certainly had plenty of them knocking at her door, but so far the 'challenge' hadn't delivered anything worthwhile.

Freddie had tried to convince his friend on several occasions that she too was perceived as a 'challenge', but for a completely different reason. As he saw it these shallow and self-centred loafers weren't interested in anything above her neckline, and certainly not looking for a 'relationship'.

He really struggled to understand her seemingly pointless obsession with these 'yobs', but it did hold certain benefits for him as he got to be her champion, the friend who was always there to help pick up the pieces when it all went wrong, an increasingly frequent occurrence as it seemed that lately she'd been gifted the knack of choosing boyfriends very badly.

Tonight he had the chance to be that hero again.

Andy, the latest, had recently been quite unpleasant and offensive to Lisa when she'd continued to refuse an invitation to go back to his flat for a 'bit of fun'. She liked 'bad' but wouldn't put up with 'nasty', so tonight she was going to confront him and dump him, then meet up with her reliable friend Freddie for a bit of moral support.

Freddie was hoping there would be tears, and imagined a chance to lend her a shoulder to cry on, another opportunity to feel her warmth, her softness. But he immediately felt guilty about his selfishness.

Taking another gulp of his beer he looked over toward the clock by the bar where John had recently installed the latest digital gadget. It was so bright it could cut through the densest fog the smokers could create, and in big red numbers it read 6:10pm.

He was guessing the wait would still be another hour at least.

"Hello Freddie, I'm skint and waiting for me giro, fancy buying me a drink?"

He instantly knew the voice, but as he turned round to look at her he didn't recognise the face, and certainly not the body.

"Karen? Karen Symonds?"

His expression didn't hide his surprise.

"Yes Freddie, Karen Symonds. Have I changed that much?" She laughed loudly.

"Surely you must remember the girl you groped in year nine?"

He didn't recognise her at all, as physically she was totally different from the short, chubby fourteen year old girl with quite bad acne he remembered from school. She was also gifted with the most magnificent breasts, certainly the biggest in the year, and if she liked you then you could get a quick feel of them in the cloakroom in the lunch break. That made her very popular with the boys and Freddie had been quick to join in the fun as often as it had been offered.

"I obviously remembered the voice."

He could feel himself blushing at the groping reference because it had been made loud enough for the whole room to hear. He grabbed her sleeve, pulled her down to sit on the seat next to him and leant in closer.

"But the bits you let me feel are all covered up. How was I supposed to recognise them?" he whispered.

"So you never looked at my face then Freddie. Typical." She laughed again, "It's okay to squeeze my tits but not remember what I look like?"

"Well you didn't look like this back then." He gestured up and down with an open hand towards her.

"You're much taller and...and prettier than I remember."

He'd almost said 'a lot thinner and less spotty' but realised that might be a little too honest and tactless.

She gave him a huge grin.

"No wonder you're always surrounded by the

13

girlies Freddie, you're such a charmer. So how about that drink? Buy me a rum and coke and I might let you discover if anything else about me has changed."

She'd hardly finished the sentence and he was already off to the bar.

When he'd returned they'd chatted excitedly for ages, recalling their shared memories of school. Karen told him stories of some of the things the boys had done just for the chance to feel her breasts.

"I told geeky Dave Harkinson that if he bought me a bar of chocolate every day for two weeks he could see them. When the time came he got so worked up that he passed out as I unbuttoned my blouse."

"Really? Must have been a rush of blood away from his brain. But I don't remember you demanding chocolate or anything else like that from me."

"I liked you Freddie, you were allowed to touch for free."

"And everyone else had to pay?"

"Listen, my folks weren't well off and I didn't get any pocket money or anything. So when these came along," she cupped her hands under her boobs, "I found out exactly how to use them. Why do you think I was chubby back then? It was all the chocolate I was given."

"Sounds like you had a proper little growing business going on."

"What are you suggesting you cheeky bugger, it wasn't anything like that. It was just a bit of harmless fun."

Their boisterous bouts of laughter were attracting some inquisitive stares from some of the closer tables.

"Shush," Freddie suddenly exclaimed.

"We best keep it down a bit, that's geeky Dave Harkinson over there."

He was really enjoying her company and it seemed mutual. With her magnificent breasts dominating the conversation Freddie's hormones were building to the point where his sexually frustrated teenage brain was starting to imagine the possibility of reliving the delights of the school cloakroom, after all it was Christmas, a time of excitement whilst unwrapping things.

"So now you've had me on the game and selling my body since I was fourteen Freddie, tell me what you do."

"I'm still at college, doing 'A' levels."

"I already guessed that bit. What are you going to be when you grow up?"

"Taller I hope, but failing that I'll settle for irresistible to women."

She tilted her head to one side and frowned.

"Maybe I should have said if you grow up Freddie, as if you boys ever do."

"Okay, you can put that look away," he relented. "I've just received an offer of a place at drama school." Fixing his eyes on her face to see her reaction he added, "I want to get into musical theatre...professionally."

For as long as he could remember Freddie had wanted to be a performer and was considered to be exceptionally gifted by those who shared this knowledge. Some of his friends knew he took part in the occasional 'out of town' play or musical, but few of them were aware just how good he was, and that he intended to pursue a career in the performing arts.

So this part of his life remained concealed to all but his family, and Lisa of course, at least until now it would seem.

"Really? That sounds great. Is it local?"

"Oxford, so it's not too far away, and it's one of the best," he said, trying to justify the situation.

"I'm sure it is and I hope you get in."

"So you're not going to take the piss and tell me I'm delusional or something?"

"Why would I do that?"

"Others have, that's why I'm usually reluctant to say anything."

"Who care what any of these losers think?" she shouted, as if to chastise the whole room. Fortunately Noddy Holder had drowned out the remark as the juke box announced, 'IT'S CHRISTMAS,' at full volume, precisely at the right moment to save Freddie's embarrassment.

"I think it must be great to have a dream and possess the talent to be able to go after it," she added.

"Thank you."

"And real friends wouldn't make fun of it." She'd raised her voice again. "So maybe you need to get some new friends."

Freddie quickly grabbed her hand.

"Erm...Yes, thanks," he gabbled, desperate to remain anonymous. "I'm sure I'll find lots of new and better friends when I get there."

Karen lifted her glass.

"So the pretty one you're always with, your girlfriend, what does she think about you going away to drama school?" she asked, taking a sip of her drink.

"Lisa? Oh she's not my girlfriend, we're not

together."

"Well, from what I've seen you should be."

"Why does everyone go on about how we should 'be together'?" he protested a little sharper than intended. "What could you possibly have seen when there's nothing to see?"

"Hey, lighten up Freddie, this is my local as well and I see you and the pretty one together in here all the time. I thought there was something going on, that's all. But if you say not, well..."

"I'm sorry," he said, now feeling a little awkward. "We're just good friends, nothing more."

"In that case." Karen dropped her chin and looked down at her ample chest, then lifted her eyes to look straight into his and gave him a cheeky smile.

"My offer to rediscover these still stands. We can go back to my flat and have a bit of fun, if you fancy."

For a second or two Freddie was mesmerised by the thought of what she was suggesting. A chance for his share a little random meaningless sex maybe? What else could she mean by 'back to her flat for a bit of fun'?

With that he suddenly remembered why he was there.

He'd been so engrossed that he'd totally forgotten about Lisa.

He turned to look over at John's digital clock again, it read 7:08pm and she should be arriving soon. Surely 'a bit of fun with Karen' couldn't be meaningless, or fun, if he let his best friend down.

"But if you've got other plans that's fine," he heard Karen say.

"Erm, I'm not really..."

He hesitated and took a large gulp of his beer.

Karen poked him hard on the arm and laughed.

"Relax Freddie, I won't bite. How about you stand me another rum and coke as a Christmas present and I'll promise to be gentle with you."

She finished off her drink and held out the glass.

"It's a deal," he said quickly, thankful for an opportunity to get away and think.

"I just hope I can afford it." He stood and headed into the smog.

"I think the bar is this way, at least I hope it is."

"You better not keep me waiting long Freddie Hobbs," she called after him. "Or I might see if someone around here fancies buying me some chocolate."

"And another pint Freddie?"

John put the rum and coke down on the bar and picked a clean glass off the rack.

"Just a half please mate, bit strapped for cash tonight."

"You're looking very thoughtful lad, everything alright?" John sounded genuinely concerned.

"I think so. I'm just a bit mixed up in my head at the moment, that's all."

"Because of her?" John nodded toward where Karen was waiting for him. Freddie turned and noticed she was talking to a tall scruffy bloke standing to the side of her table.

"Be careful young Freddie, don't get mixing with the wrong crowd."

"What do you mean?"

"Just friendly counsel lad, nothing more. But tell me, when you got up this morning were you happy?"

"I reckon so, yes."

"Then just remember which bed you got out of. A different one tonight could make things so complicated it might even ruin the rest of your life."

He put a pint of bitter down on the counter. "There's a lesson there for everyone I think, and this one's on the house."

As Freddie got back to the table Karen was yelling at the scruffy bloke.

"Oh just piss off Ronnie."

Scruffy turned to walk away.

"All right mate," he said, smiling at Freddie. Then plodding away from the table he disappeared into the fog.

"Who's Ronnie?" Freddie asked, putting the drinks down.

Karen was shredding a beer mat, her cheeks were flushed and tears rimmed her eyes.

"Ronnie's a wanker, one of Ryan's idiot mates," she mumbled.

"Ryan? Is that your boyfriend?" Freddie asked warily. Her outburst at Ronnie had attracted more attention from the nearby tables again and he really didn't want to agitate the situation.

Karen wiped her face and took a sip of her drink.

"Ryan was my useless boyfriend. We've been living together for a year, but now the week before soddin' Christmas, he's suddenly buggered off to be with someone else. Never even bothered to say goodbye, just took our savings and left."

She screwed up what was left of the beer mat and threw it on the floor.

"Apparently he's told that tosser Ronnie to look out for me, you know, keep an eye on me. Who the hell does he think he is?"

Freddie felt really sorry for her, a seemingly nice person who'd been let down by an idiot. It was in his nature to want to help, but he just didn't know what to say, and after John's comments he didn't want to get involved either, certainly not with the likes of Ryan and Ronnie.

His shoulders slumped in response to his thoughts, his body language betraying a growing sense of awkwardness.

Karen had noticed.

"I'm sorry," she said. "Things have been a bit shitty lately. I just wanted a bit of friendly company for a change and you always seem so cheerful."

She picked up her drink and finished it in one.

"Thanks for the drink Freddie."

"I'm sorry too, but..."

"It's okay I understand, another time maybe." She stood, then bent down and kissed him on the cheek. "Be honest with that pretty girl of yours Freddie, everyone else has noticed except you. Tell her how you feel, you'll be surprised."

"Or it just might ruin everything and she never speaks to me again."

He felt himself blush at the sudden realisation that for the very first time he'd admitted his feelings to someone else, and almost a stranger at that.

"I'm glad you came over," he said. "And I hope things work out for you."

Karen smiled.

"There's something about you Freddie Hobbs that cheers a girl up no matter what."

She kissed him again and was gone.

7.28pm - "She looked very pretty you lucky lad. Anything you want to tell me?"

Lisa arrived at the table just seconds after Karen had left.

"John's sent you another pint," she added, setting it down on the table. "And I got a large Bacardi 'on the house'. He said Happy Christmas."

She moved her stool right next to him, sat down, hugged his arm and kissed him on his cheek, as she always did.

"Come on then, spill the beans," she insisted.

"There's nothing to tell," he said defensively.

"Someone from school came over to say hello."

"And?"

"And, that's all."

"You were looking very thoughtful when I got here, and John said you seemed troubled about something." She started playfully tormenting the side of his ribs with her fingers.

"You know you'll have to tell me eventually."

Freddie laughed and grabbed her hand to stop the harassment of his body.

"Okay, okay, I'll tell you, even though there's absolutely nothing to tell."

He took a gulp of beer and wondered just how much he should reveal, more importantly how much detail of the encounter would satisfy Lisa's curiosity. He certainly didn't want to admit anything compromising to the girl he idolised.

Trust John to stir an empty pot.

"Her boyfriend had dumped her and she was just looking for a bit of friendly company. I felt sorry for her and bought her a drink, nothing more exciting than that."

"You're such a sweetie Freddie, always wanting to help."

"But only pretty people, ugly folk can sort out their own problems."

"Well she was very pretty, do you like her?" Lisa enquired, picking up her drink and taking a sip.

"She was nice, yes I liked her."

"That was past tense Freddie, aren't you going to see her again?" She took another sip.

"I doubt it. We had very little in common. She was only looking for a bit of fun."

"Oh...Oh I see."

Freddie failed to notice the brief smile that flashed across his best friends face.

"Talking of which," he said, desperate to deflect Lisa's interest away from his encounter with Karen.

"Tell me all the gossip about you and 'Bad Boy' Andy. How did it go?"

"Well, unsurprisingly he'd forgotten we'd arranged to meet at the office. He wasn't there."

"His office! When did he get a job?"

"A job! Don't be daft Freddie."

She punched his arm.

"The burger bar on Dowel Street, it's called 'The Office', and Andy spends all day in there playing the video machine."

"Sorry, I forgot. It must be all this free beer." He took a gulp. "At least it numbs the pain in my arm."

Lisa punched him again, but gently.

"Anyway," she continued, "I was hungry so I got myself a chicken sandwich and waited. Fifteen minutes later he strolls in with some rough looking tart round his neck, trying to chew one of his ears off."

"Classy."

"Anyway there's not a lot more to say really, but I'll give you the highlights."

She giggled. "It was all really hilarious."

Freddie was a little disappointed that she didn't seem upset about any of this at all, quite the opposite.

"So I go over and politely enquire as to why he'd forgotten our date and requested the identity of the gnawing female. The tart yells 'who the hell is this?' and added 'so this is why you keep standing me up' and smacks his face. Andy grunts an unintelligent reply, shrugs his shoulders and heads over to the video machine. Big mistake because the tart grabs two of those plastic sauce bottles off the nearest table and squirts it all over the back of his prized leather jacket, then picks up a half eaten burger that someone's left and tries to shove it down his neck. I'm still holding a chocolate milkshake and it seemed only natural to pour it over his head."

"I bet he looked a right mess."

"Yeah, just like a human happy meal."

They leant against each other as they chuckled like kids.

"I'm glad I waited for him," Lisa added, "It was so worth it."

"But was it worth a whole chocolate milk shake?" Freddie asked. "Banana yellow might have been a better choice."

Now they were both in hysterics.

"I'm really happy you're back to being single again," Freddie suddenly blurted out. "Erm...I mean happy you're not with Andy anymore that is," he quickly added, hoping that would conceal what he'd really meant.

"Oh yes, and what's that supposed to mean?" Lisa quizzed.

"Nothing, I'm just saying."

Freddie picked up his pint, feeling a little embarrassed by his unguarded declaration.

Lisa hugged his arm again and rested her chin on his shoulder, a big soppy grin covered her face.

"But what are you saying exactly?"

He felt himself start to redden up, his mind torn on whether to tell her or not. He was suddenly struck with the thought that the way she acted towards him sometimes might suggest that John and Karen were right, or were they merely misinterpreting her friendliness?

Her closeness was certainly warming more than just his arm.

"I just think that for the likes of Andy it's all a game," he said instead.

"A game?"

"A video game, a contest to discover a way to plunder the hidden treasure."

"I've never heard it called that before."

"Maybe not but you knew exactly what I meant."

Lisa chuckled at his analogy.

"Go on," she said, unwrapping her arm from his and sitting back.

He immediately missed her.

"Erm, well that's it really. These 'Bad Boys' see girlfriends as the latest video game, and when a new adventure with undiscovered features comes along they just have to pursue it. Then as soon as the quest for the hidden treasure is completed, and the bonus play taken, they usually lose interest and move on to the next level."

Lisa started laughing loudly. "You know Freddie Hobbs, your ideas often walk a tightrope of silliness over an abyss of insanity. I think that one just fell off."

"Cheek, and there was me thinking you 'ladies' loved a wit."

"Carry on like that and you'll be 'lady-less' for the rest of your life."

Now they were both in hysterics again. When Freddie could finally breathe he took a gulp of beer.

"With any luck I'll still have one really good friend though," he said.

"Of course you will, John the Manager loves everyone," she teased.

"Oh thanks a lot, but he's really not my type."

"Are you sure about that?"

She started probing his ribs with her fingers again. "With all the free beer and concern for your well being I reckon you two have a bit of a 'man thing' going on."

"He reckons he's a bit of a 'Bad Boy' so he's more your type than mine."

"After Andy I'm not really sure I know what my type is anymore," she said thoughtfully. "Tell me honestly why you're happy I broke up with him."

"He wasn't good for you, and certainly not what you want."

"How can you be so sure of that?"

"Well if Andy, or the other leather jacketed, wannabe biker type, 'no job no hopers' had been exactly what you wanted, you wouldn't have spent so long being a lifestyle missionary to them all."

"Lifestyle missionary?"

"Yeah, trying to convert them into something they'll never be."

"What's that?"

"Interesting."

"Fair enough," she said and put her arm back through his.

"Come on then, you know me better than anyone else, what do I want and where can I find it?"

"You should start with someone who knows words of more than one syllable and can actually hold a conversation about the things you're interested in."

"Good start, I like that."

"You need someone who wants to be with you for who you are and not just what they can get from you."

"Getting better."

"Let's give him a sensitive side and he'll actually have plans for the future, a future to share together."

"Now you've gone from possible to unlikely, that's asking way too much," she said sarcastically. "But go on, I'm interested to know more about this ideal man you're creating for me."

"In my opinion you deserve someone who'll be your best friend and never let you down, that's certainly nothing like Andy or his type."

"I hope this person comes along soon and asks me out, he sounds perfect."

"You think?...I don't."

"You already have someone in mind don't you?" Her face lit up with a huge smile and her eyes crinkled in the corners.

"Who is it Freddie, tell me, tell me."

He hesitated, too afraid to say the words. He

really wanted to, but was he about to lose everything?

But then how long could he go on just waiting and wondering. A month, a year, a lifetime?

"Well I was hoping," he hesitated and took a deep breath.

"It could be me."

Two

<u>November 2013</u>

Tuesday 26th 7.30 am - Freddie unlocked the stage door and pushed it open, but as he stepped inside it felt like the damp morning mist was pulling at him from behind.

    Although this unusually early start to his day was exceptionally annoying, it wasn't the only reason for his dark mood, which stubbornly clung to him like the swirling grey vapour he'd stumbled through from the car park. After closing the door behind him he paused for a minute, allowing his eyes to adjust to the ever present blackness of the back stage area, and after blinking hard for a second or two he was ready to move on, desperate to dispel the unwelcome frustration he was currently experiencing and dislodge the tightening grip of his annoying little worry monkey.

    There were no windows in this area of the theatre but Freddie never turned on any lights when he was here on his own. No matter what time of day it was, he always preferred the dark, it forced him to focus and concentrate more on navigating his way around using his other senses, and today this would be a convenient distraction.

"There's a lot you can hide from in the dark, eh monkey," he muttered.

Freddie rarely had much to worry about, but for the first time in nearly thirteen years there was upset in his seemingly perfect marriage to the lovely Lisa.

What had started as a mere concern at the back of his mind had been allowed to fester without any logical reason. He'd tried to ignore this 'worry monkey' but his overactive imagination was gradually persuading him that a crisis might be looming on the horizon.

Lisa had always been an extremely focused individual and most definitely the organiser in their relationship, possessing the determination to get exactly what she wanted out of life, and knowing precisely how and when it should happen.

Totally unlike Freddie, who was somewhat more relaxed about almost everything.

Away from his demanding role at the theatre, he was content to sit back and just let things happen around him, and because of Lisa they did. For many years he'd enjoyed a life made so much easier because his lovely wife made all of the important decisions, and he was keen for this arrangement to continue.

"Whatever it takes to keep her happy is fine by me," was definitely a phrase used often, and he went to great pains to ensure that his lovely Lisa felt her efforts to create the perfect home were properly appreciated. It had obviously worked well because everyone could see they enjoyed a very content and harmonious union.

As the senior partner and editor in chief of IG Lifestyle, a small but very popular up-market fashion magazine, Lisa was fanatically attentive about her appearance. She kept fit at the gym, generally ate healthily and was very particular about her hair and make-up.

In her professional role she had acquired a talent for finding and showcasing the newest designers and giving exposure to the latest fashions, directing her readership from yesterday's fad to a better and more modern look. Her much acclaimed and sought after endorsement of current lifestyle trends came with some distinct advantages and Freddie would often come home to find the entire house temporarily remodelled in 'must have' designer furniture, ready for an in depth article and photo-shoot. Then there were the samples, such as wardrobes full of clothes and shoes, kitchen accessories and the very latest 'how did we ever live without one of these' gadgets, all freely 'loaned' for the chance to get a few words of recommendation in IG Lifestyle.

And when it came to the more intimate issues, even the advice about 'How to Have Great Sex' had been thoroughly tried and tested at home before publication, a task in which Freddie was always a willing participant. This lucky lad enjoyed the very best of everything with very little effort on his part. His stunningly sexy wife, who loved him to bits, ensured his every moment with her was a wonderful experience.

He considered his life was just perfect.

But now this 'career woman' had a new plan.

She'd achieved a great deal of her ambitions professionally and the time had come to answer a call from nature.

Lisa wanted a baby.

When his wonderful wife wanted something Freddie had always done his best to ensure it happened. On this occasion he'd been even more obliging than usual, enthusiastic and willing to put his heart, soul and a few other body parts into action in the interest of marital harmony and the happiness of his soul mate.

But a year had passed and for some reason the plan wasn't working, and as each month passed unsuccessfully Lisa's frustration was starting to emerge. Initially there had been some light hearted bickering between them, but now it had escalated to a point where she was eager to discover a cause for the failure, and she had a prime suspect.

That same morning Freddie had been buttering a mound of toast in the kitchen when she'd burst into the room.

"I've been telling you fruit for breakfast instead of all that carbohydrate," she'd snapped.

He noticed she'd been crying and instantly suspected it was because another unsuccessful month had passed, and she still wasn't pregnant.

"I'm sorry," he'd said. Putting the butter knife down he'd walked towards her, holding out his arms to give her a reassuring cuddle, but she'd deftly sidestepped him and headed for the sink.

"I don't want sympathy Freddie, I want a baby." She'd noisily started filling the bowl with crockery, hopeful that the clattering of plates would hide the tremor in her voice.

"I'm never going to get pregnant without a bit more effort from you Freddie."

"Oh come on sweetie, there's been no lack of effort from either of us and it'll happen when it happens. You can't plan the details, nature makes up its own mind."

"It's been a year already Freddie, how much longer can we afford to wait?" She'd yelled and banged a mug down on the drainer. "Another year? Two? Five? We can't wait for nature Freddie, we're running out of time...I'm running out of time."

He'd really wanted to hug her and tell her everything would be just fine, but knew she wouldn't let him. He wasn't prepared to be drawn into a senseless argument over apportioning blame for something that couldn't be helped either, so retreat rather than confrontation was by far the better option. He'd picked up his coat, grabbed a piece of toast from the top of the pile and quickly headed for the door.

"Please wait up for me tonight and I'll get away early, we'll have a good long talk about this."

He'd spoken quickly so she couldn't fire back a reply.

He'd reached the door.

"You know I'll do whatever you want," he'd added, hoping this would be enough to placate her for now. He was sure everything would be okay if they both had some time to reflect on the situation.

"Anything?" she'd snapped, snatching up a towel to dry her hands. "Okay then Freddie, let's talk later and we'll see if you really mean that."

His shoulders slumped as he turned to walk out

of the door, but he hesitated. He couldn't go like this, not until he was sure she knew.

"I love you," he'd said, then held his breath, worried she wouldn't reply.

Her voice was quiet and sounded a bit croaky, like she'd started crying again,

"I love you too."

Freddie was still standing in the pitch black of the scenery dock trying to put the earlier events at home into perspective, something he'd always try to do. But unfortunately it was taking much longer than usual for the calming nature of these familiar surroundings to take effect.

From the moment he'd arrived for a job interview in '98 he'd loved this theatre. It felt right, it even smelt right and at a point in his life where the present had been traumatic and the future unclear it became a solid and welcome lifeline. He'd certainly spent more time here in the last sixteen years than anywhere else and he counted his work colleagues as some of his closest friends, almost family...well most of them anyway.

He'd started as a stage technician but then quickly worked his way up the very short ladder, his attitude and work ethic impressing the trustees as he went. So when the old Technical and Stage Manager retired two years later Freddie was the natural choice as his successor.

For him it was the best job in the world.

Arriving companies would carry their dreams and expectations onto his stage, where his experience and knowledge would help them to create a world of wonder for the paying public to enjoy.

For Freddie the theatre is pure fantasy and the perfect place for anybody to escape from the harsh realities of life, and it didn't matter to him if there was a show going on or not. The magic was always there, every time he crossed the threshold he could feel it.

But today he hadn't been able to leave his worries outside that big heavy stage door as usual, and as it had snapped shut and the shadows cast by the morning light had disappeared, only the grey swirling mist had been left behind. His lovely Lisa wanted this baby so badly that she wasn't being her normal self. Sense told him that given time she would realise that, and she needed to be patient.

.....*'Unless of course there's a problem'*.....

Said his worry monkey.

Lisa's rare show of angry frustration was allowing worry to poke at the tiny cracks in Freddie's imagination, opening them up a little more. He couldn't deny there was doubt, and it was a painful thought because with it came 'what if?' That was something he really didn't want to consider.

.....*'Oh come on Freddie, after a year and all that sex, there must be a problem. I bet Lisa thinks there's a problem'*.....

"There's no point in worrying about something we can't be certain of," he suddenly said out loud. "She's a smart girl and everything will be fine, so come on Freddie my boy, it's time to get the kettle on."

.....*'The problem won't just go away Freddie'*.....

"You can try little monkey, like you've tried before, but you'll never win because I know your game. So you might as well just bugger off. Right now I've got another minor irritation requiring some attention."

He squared his shoulders and set off in the dark carefully picking a route through the scenery dock. He made his way toward the green room and started to focus on the priorities of the day ahead.

"Coffee and Neil in that order and I'll worry about my lovely Lisa later."

Yesterday, Neil a visiting first aid trainer had delivered the first part of a three day course for all the employed staff at THCT (The Hidden Theatre Company)

Unfortunately, the only space in the venue which was large enough to use for practical training purposes was on the stage itself. Neil, obviously aware of where he was, had appeared determined to put on a comedy performance worthy of the setting, attempting to turn each and every topic into a comedy routine, with innuendo liberally thrown in for good measure. With his very own captive audience he'd wanted to share all of his personal experiences since childhood in minute detail. He had a quip for everything and had started nearly every other sentence with, "Something funny happened when I…"

The problem was that none of his anecdotes seemed remotely relevant to the course, and they certainly weren't funny. The staff, having given up their own time to learn this important skill had been bored, patience was wearing thin and moods were darkening.

As the 'Boss' Freddie was in early today to try and sort things out.

Two strong black coffees and twenty minutes

later, Freddie was feeling a little more like himself. He'd made two more mugs of coffee and filled the thermos ready for when the rest of the staff arrived.

Just as he'd hoped Neil was early, this would be the perfect opportunity to offer a little friendly advice before the situation got any worse.

"Morning Neil." He held up one of the steaming mugs and beckoned Neil over as he walked into the green room. "Two sugars if I've remembered rightly, here you go chap."

Freddie called everyone he liked 'mate' and reserved 'chap' for those who annoyed him.

"Great, thanks," Neil said. He took the drink and warmed his hands around the mug.

"I was looking around last night after clearing my stuff away, it must be great fun working here Freddie, got any vacancies?"

"It's like any job Neil, seems glamorous from the outside, but we work very long hours, often without thanks and always to a very tight schedule. Talking of which..."

"Don't you just hate these cold damp mornings?" Neil interrupted.

"Especially as for us the morning is usually at the end of our working day, not the beginning. Talking of which..."

"Definitely not my favourite part of the day either," Neil interrupted again. "But..."

"Sorry Neil," this time it was Freddie's turn to interrupt. "But I just need to remind you that all six of us are attending this training in our own time, and being here at this ridiculous hour in the morning isn't good for lightening the mood of my exhausted staff. We understand that this is important and that's why we're here, but I must say we're..."

"Having a great laugh with me," Neil butted in again. "Yeah I know that already Freddie, but thanks for telling me. Everyone has fun on my courses, it's definitely been worth getting up early for, don't you think?"

Freddie struggled to think of an honest but diplomatic answer. This time-wasting idiot had to be told to stop messing about, but he would never be rude no matter how much he was provoked.

He'd just have to start again.

"Sorry we all ran off last night but we had a lot to get done before the show."

"That's okay, I'll soon get through the stuff we missed."

"Good, but I just want to make sure we don't have any more delays or distractions today so I thought I might have a quiet word before we start."

"Certainly Freddie, how about silence? That's the quietest word I know."

"What? Oh yes, very funny, but it's your natural hilarity I want talk about."

"So you think I'm a natural then?"

"Most definitely," Freddie coughed the lie. "But you must understand we have professional comedians here at the theatre all the time, and because we're not allowed to laugh backstage humour is lost on us. We don't get it Neil, we're not allowed to get it, so there's no point trying. So you might as well cut out the jokes."

"But like you say I'm naturally funny, the humour just floods out of me and I can't help myself. This would be a much happier place to be if I worked here, I'd fit in well and cheer you all up."

"And I'm sure we'd be eternally grateful, but until then can we just concentrate on the first aid and maybe we won't run out of time like we did yesterday. You said we've still got a lot to cover so forget the jokes Neil, it'll save time and we won't be hurting your feelings when we don't laugh."

"Oh don't worry about my feelings Freddie. I continually amaze myself at how funny I am, and that makes me feel great."

"Just the first aid please Neil. This can be a dangerous place and I need the staff to be confident enough to handle any emergency."

"I find a joke always lightens any situation."

"Well I'm not sure humour would work in the 'Sorry I couldn't remember how to do CPR on your husband Mrs Smith but he died with the one about the gorilla on the golf course ringing in his ears' situation."

"They say the hearing is the last thing to fail, so nothing wrong with..."

"Neil," Freddie said, gritting his teeth to stop himself from shouting.

"The course assessment is at four tomorrow afternoon and there's still a load of stuff to cover from yesterday. We can't afford to fall behind today so you need to crack on chap, no jokes, no stories, just first aid. I'll not be very happy if anybody fails. Are we clear on this?"

Freddie picked up his mug and turned to head for the office.

"Yes, but hang on a minute," Neil called after him, "Can I just ask you one favour."

Freddie turned to face him, Neil looked genuinely excited.

"What?" he barked.

"I'm always looking for new material to use, please tell me the one about the gorilla on the golf course."

8.50 am - As the rest of the staff arrived for the day they were gathering in the green room for their morning coffee, while Neil the trainer got everything set up and ready on the stage.

"Were you your usual nice self Freddie, or did you tell him straight?" Brian the Front of House Manager asked sarcastically.

"I tried diplomacy Brian but I think he's as thick as he is dull. Neil's one of these people who just wants to be liked and uses the comedy routine to impress."

"But he's not the slightest bit funny boss."

Steve, the Fly Captain and stage fight co-ordinator, was munching his way through a whole packet of stale digestives. "I've seen you laugh at jelly but you've not cracked a smile yet."

"Maybe asking him to work on the stage was an invitation he couldn't resist," Brian offered. "Give anyone a voice on a stage and they soon turn into a right diva."

"He was a diva before he started. I've told him to tone down the theatrics but I'm fairly certain he wasn't listening, loves the sound of his own voice does that one. Just look at this, what's he up to now?"

Freddie was pointing at the show relay monitor in the corner of the room which he'd switched on out of habit. It clearly showed Neil standing in the middle of the stage facing the empty stalls with his head high and arms flung wide.

"Turn it up boss."

Freddie reached up and increased the volume.

"Thank you, thank you."

Neil's voice echoed around the auditorium. Then he started bowing to the imaginary crowd, unaware of the camera and microphone in the auditorium picking up his every action.

"What a fool," Steve laughed.

"Oh come on Steve," Freddie said. "We've all done that at one time or another. I can remember a certain member of my crew stripping off to Tom Jones's 'You can leave your hat on' when he thought he was here all alone one night."

"You know I was rehearsing for an audition," Steve protested. "He's just an idiot."

"I think he's quite cute, typically my type." Brian was still staring at the screen.

"Anything male with a pulse is your type Brian," Steve said spraying digestive crumbs everywhere. "But I'm certain you're nowhere near his type, he's much more interested in the new girl from the box office."

"Just let me get him in the props room and he'll soon change his type."

Freddie nearly choked on his coffee.

"There'll be no more prop room incidents thank you." He reached up and switched off the monitor.

"Come on, Scotty's here now. Go and get the girls from the office please Bri and let's get started, the quicker we get going the quicker we'll be rid of Neil. Oh and just a word of caution."

Freddie had just remembered something important he must tell them.

"No one is to mention the volunteer programme either, otherwise we'll be stuck with him."

"I still wouldn't mind getting stuck to him."

"No mention Brian or else, and the props room is off limits to you for the rest of today, no make that forever."

As soon as the two managers were out of sight Steve opened another packet of biscuits and took a handful.

"What happened in the props room?"

Scotty, the youngest member of the stage crew, was pouring the last of the coffee all over the table as he tipped the thermos flask up and the lid fell off.

"Brian took advantage of the pantomime dame at an after show party a couple of years ago."

Steve sprayed another shower of digestive crumbs all over the junior stage hand.

"In the props room?"

"Yep, then they set off the smoke detectors with a post shag fag and the stage drenchers opened up. Took days to dry out the drapes, good job we had a maintenance week booked before the next show."

"What did management say?"

"Nothing, Freddie covered for him. Brian should have lost his job really but the boss is a good bloke, he told management we'd had an electrical fault in a scanner. There was no real damage and we didn't lose revenue so no one made a fuss. Anyway we can't stand around here all day drinking coffee, let's get going. If you remember I'm dying to make a fool out of Neil the git today, come on this is going to be fun."

9.00 am - Once everyone was seated Neil began.

"Morning everyone, busy day today so let's get started." He paused and put a big smile on his face. "So did you all go home last night and practice your bondage, oops sorry my mistake, I meant bandaging. Bet you lot never thought a bit of first aid could spice things up in the bedroom?"

"We all worked really late Neil," Freddie said. "By the time I got home even the cat had gone to bed."

"Were you planning on bandaging the cat then Freddie? I remember something funny happened when I..."

"Neil," Freddie cut in. "Is this story relevant?" He wanted to stop any nonsense before it started.

"Yes definitely! It's all about when I tried to bandage up my cat, so funny."

"We'll take your word as to the relevance of bandaging a cat to first aid and how funny you think we'll find it. But as you said, we have a lot to get through so can we move on please?"

"You brought up the cat Freddie so I thought you might like to hear how funny it is to try bandaging one."

"I can't imagine why I would need to bandage a cat, or why it would be remotely funny."

"I promise you'll laugh yourself silly, it's a really good story."

"We have a saying in the theatre Neil which I think could be very significant in this situation."

"I love sayings, what is it?"

"Just stick to the script...forget about bandaging a cat."

"Wow, that's amazing."

"What is?"

"The fact we were talking about bandaging a cat and you actually have a saying 'Forget about bandaging a cat' that's just mind blowing."

Freddie threw up his hands in frustration, this was going nowhere fast and by bantering with this nut he was just making the situation worse.

"Neil, what topic are we covering this morning?" he asked calmly.

"Well you're supposed to practice more bandaging to control severe bleeding and then we'll talk about burns and fractures."

"I think we all got the bandaging right yesterday." He addressed the others, "Are we all happy with bandaging?" Everybody nodded.

"Let's move on to burns then, please."

"But I was going to get you each to bandage a part of Scotty for practice, trust me it is hilarious turning someone into a mummy. Something funny happened last time I..."

"Neil, if we can make it to the coffee break without any more 'funny happenings' I'll be so grateful that I won't let Steve and Scotty fly you right to the top of grid at lunchtime as they're planning."

"Oh Boss," Steve slumped in his chair and scowled.

"I told you he wouldn't let us do it," Scotty said to his co-conspirator.

"It actually sounds quite good fun, I'm up for it," Neil said excitedly.

"It stops being fun when they abandon you up there for an hour and the harness makes your legs go numb for a week, that was their plan," Freddie revealed.

"BOSS."

Steve was disappointed.

"We thought it would give him a great story to tell on his next course, you know...Something funny happened at the theatre when I pissed off the crew once too often. He'd definitely get a few laughs for that one."

Neil was looking affronted, but Freddie wasn't going to give the trainer any chance to respond and waste even more time.

"Burns and fractures please chap. Trust me the flying harness plays havoc with your sex life."

Neil agreed it was time to move on.

12.30 pm – Everyone was enjoying a well deserved lunch break

The rest of the morning session had been better except for one inappropriate moment. During the discussion about possible causes of friction burns Neil had commented that surely they'd all experienced carpet burns, the ladies on their buttocks and the lads on their knees.

No one had laughed, and Neil's smile quickly vanished to be replaced by a look of disappointment when Freddie had suggested his comments were inappropriate with Ann and Amy present.

Freddie wasn't a prude but he didn't appreciate anyone being crude on his stage.

During the break Freddie made sure Steve and Scotty fully understood his instructions and wouldn't do anything to the unsuspecting Neil.

"No flying Steve, I don't want him vomiting on the stage from the top of the grid."

"What height can I make him vomit from then?"

"You know what I mean. I don't want any kit

damaged and I certainly don't want blue flashing lights around when the house opens tonight."

"He's still a git and deserves some payback."

"Maybe he does but not that way Steve. It's way too risky and we don't have the time."

Steve wouldn't cross this particular line and Freddie knew it. But there had been a lot of huddles and whispering during lunch and he was worried there could be other plans going on.

It wouldn't be the first time the staff would be looking to retaliate, and he wouldn't blame them if they did.

Three

5.00 pm – The afternoon session had been much better than Freddie was expecting and it seemed that he may have been wrong about Steve and Scotty planning something after all.

Surprisingly Neil was quite subdued as well and at last things seemed to have settled down. They even got to practice CPR on a naked female manikin without any jokes or suggestive comments from anyone.

With the training finished for the day Freddie had an important regular appointment to keep, so headed off to the Lotus Leaf Cantonese Diner, a small Chinese restaurant close to the theatre, to meet up with his Uncle Roy.

For many years Royston Hobbs had been a well known and respected managing agent in the entertainment industry, and was specifically appreciated by a countless number of once hungry performing artists whom he'd represented well for a meagre twenty percent.

Back in May '95 he'd signed an exceptionally talented eighteen year old performer, his nephew Freddie Hobbs who appeared to be destined for a very bright future.

Freddie had completed his A' levels that year, achieving three excellent grades, and along with his uncle's financial support had been rewarded with the opportunity to take up the offer to study musical theatre for two years at a renowned drama school in Oxford.

His aging parents were delighted their boy was able to pursue the career he loved. They were fully supportive and had never insisted he found a 'proper job'.

Lisa was also very happy for her wonderfully attentive boyfriend, despite the fact that she knew it would mean seeing so much less of him for a while. But she needed him to go, not only to pursue his dreams but also because it allowed her to follow her own ambitions in publishing, and Freddie would just be a distraction if he stayed around.

Although she would miss his incredibly valuable support and advice, her only real concern was all those lovely female dancers he'd be working with.

He'd told her she should be more worried about some of the boys.

Freddie proved not to be just a good student but an outstanding performer, and after graduating he was immediately offered work in various professional productions. Starting in the chorus line he'd instantly gained a reputation for being a grafter and quick learner, which got him noticed by the bigger producers. Well before his twenty first birthday he was regularly being offered minor roles in some of the bigger shows.

His Mom and Dad had been so proud of him and, despite their failing health, had attended as many of his performances as they could manage.

His biggest fan, the lovely Lisa, attended as often as her work took her up to London, when they'd spend as much time together as they could find, mostly testing out the soundproofing of his latest bedsit accommodation.

Then out of the blue his big chance arrived.

A fairly new but very popular production called 'Backstage' had just finished a run in the West End, and the producers were planning a UK tour of the show.

They'd asked Freddie to take the principal lead.

Rehearsals went well and everybody involved with the production had been delighted. They had a great show, a strong talented cast and advance ticket sales were fantastic.

With the promise of good money coming in Freddie had felt it was time to ask Lisa to marry him, and Uncle Roy had put down an obscene deposit on a very flash new Bentley. His association with Freddie had extensively increased his business and anticipation was high for a very lucrative future.

For just the briefest of moments everything had seemed perfect for this rising sensation and his agent, but fate had other plans and Freddie's future was about to be dramatically altered beyond recognition.

He'd walked across the rehearsal stage a hundred times before, but for some reason during the final dress Freddie decided to fall off the apron, landing with a thud in the orchestra pit, ten feet below. To this day he has no recollection of the incident, and no idea how or why it happened.

But it did, and he managed to 'break a leg' for real, as well as three ribs and a finger.

Sadly he'd never made the opening night of 'Backstage', or any other show on any other night since, as the accident ensured he would never be able to dance again.

Overwhelmed and dejected Freddie gave up performing and went home, his confidence in tatters.

But that wasn't to be the end of his heartache as both of his elderly parents passed away during the following year, and although they left him a decent financial inheritance and a large beautiful house, a huge black hole opened up in his life.

Fortunately he still had Lisa, who'd gladly accepted his proposal. A life without her would truly have been the greatest disaster for him.

Meanwhile, Uncle Roy went back to finding talent and also managed to secure a job for Freddie at THTC, hoping that by keeping his nephew in the theatre it would rekindle his desire to perform again.

As lives and careers were rebuilt, uncle and nephew settled into a now familiar routine. Twelve times each year, on the last Tuesday of each month, the Lotus Leaf Cantonese Diner played host as the venue for a family gathering featuring the same cast of two, with a very bizarre and unchanging script.

Freddie would always arrive to find Roy already seated at their usual table, his suit jacket folded neatly and draped over the back of a spare chair, with his briefcase open on the seat. The older man would then rise and very formally and firmly shake his nephew's hand. This was the signal for the restaurant staff to quickly busy themselves, delivering hot plates and copious amounts of deliciously aromatic dim sum to the table, where it was systematically arranged with almost military precision.

Over the years Roy had become an extreme creature of obsessive habit, everything had to be orderly, punctual and precise, from the way he dressed to the position his food was laid out on the table. It was a characteristic that most of his acquaintances found exceptionally irritating, but he was very good at making money, so for those who tolerated his meticulous nature the associated benefits were well worth the occasional sacrifice of their sanity.

The manager was so familiar with this monthly routine that everything was already prepared, so by the time the pair had spoken their greetings and taken their seats a feast was laid.

And the ritual would begin.

"Glad you could make it lad."

"I'd always find time for our little get-together Uncle Roy."

He meant it.

"It all looks incredibly good as usual, let's eat."

Roy would then produce a clean white linen napkin and gold plated cutlery from his briefcase.

"I like to come prepared," he'd say, tucking the napkin into his shirt collar to protect a very expensive silk tie.

As part of the process there were even specific phrases Roy had to say, particular comments he'd made to Freddie every single month for years. They were an important part of his meticulous routine, with no malice or bitterness intended, it was just essential for him to offer an opinion and thus appease his own demons.

Freddie accepted this and had found it easier to facilitate the process quickly by leading the conversation in the right direction. Again it was all part of the familiar and well rehearsed script.

"How was the journey?" Freddie asked.

"Not too bad really, the train was quiet. Nobody uses them nowadays, but I'm not surprised as they're so mucky."

With this comment Roy reached into his case, this time a bottle of liquid hand cleanser and packet of paper hankies appeared.

"Do you mean the trains or the people?" Freddie enquired.

Roy laughed as if he'd genuinely never heard this joke told twelve times a year, then squeezed far too much of the gel into his hand.

"You should get a car again, Uncle." Freddie continued, "You could afford a chauffeur."

Roy hadn't owned a car for years, these days the roads were far too chaotic for him. He would only even consider taking a cab as a last resort, but never for more than just a few miles. Freddie knew this but his comment allowed...

"And you should perform again," Roy insisted.

He was trying desperately to get into the tightly packed tissues with slimy hands.

"The day you tread the boards again lad, I'll get a car and drive it myself. You're wasting such a great talent."

That was the first thing he needed to say.

"So you keep telling me Uncle, but you know I can't dance anymore and I'm sure my ability to hold a tune has long gone."

"How do you know if you don't try? At your age there are plenty of roles where you don't have to dance. You should at least try."

That was the second, and he'd finally managed to release the tissues.

"But as you know Uncle, we're trying for a baby I just wouldn't have the time."

Freddie was always looking for new excuses for his apparent unwillingness to return to the stage and this was the latest addition to the routine.

With his tongue poking out of the corner of his mouth, Roy was furiously rubbing his hands with the paper hankies in an attempt to remove the copious excess of the liquid gel.

"I'm not sure either of you will have enough time or patience to bring up a baby. You're just too set in your ways for such a big change to your life."

"Lisa calls it well established. A nice home with a stable relationship makes coping with change a lot easier. Apparently current thinking suggests that children of older parents are more confident and feel less insecure."

"More likely to be lonely and neglected because of older parents who are too knackered to do anything exciting or fun."

Roy was becoming quite animated and lumps of soggy tissue were flying in all directions as he waved his hands about.

"In fact forget the exciting and fun bit you'll just be too knackered to do anything." Roy laughed at his own remark.

"That's a bit unfair Uncle. My job is very physically demanding and I can keep up with someone half my age."

Freddie was finding it very hard to keep a straight face as Roy had managed to flick bits of soggy tissue everywhere. There was a lump stuck to his chin and another on his left ear.

"Just think about it lad, when your child is ten it'll be a fifth of your age and torturing you just for something fun to do. It's probably a good thing you two are just trying and not succeeding. If you ask me a baby is not a good idea at your age."

"If you remember, when I was born my Dad was a lot older that I am now and he managed okay."

"Sorry lad, I didn't mean to be disrespectful. But you should also remember you were still very young when he died."

Freddie was trying to ignore the white globular earring his uncle had acquired, but couldn't. He pointed and smirked.

"Erm sorry, you have some..." he gestured for his uncle to wipe his ear.

He needed to get back to the usual script otherwise they'd go round in circles for ever on this topic.

"Look, I promise to give the acting some serious thought Uncle."

"You're always promising to give it some thought my lad, but Lisa does all the thinking for you. That girl of yours, lovely as she is, always has other plans. Isn't it time you did what you want for a change? Be the man in your own house."

There, that was the third and last. Now they could both relax a little, and as Roy had concluded the cleaning of his hands it was time to eat.

Thank goodness for hot plates.

Roy beckoned the waiter, an older man with a weatherworn face who was leaning on a pillar nearby in anticipation of the summons.

"Two large whiskies please, and can you take this mess away, thanks."

Roy gestured at the crumpled and shredded tissues littering the table and floor. The waiter nodded an acknowledgement and fussed around picking up the clutter, but for the first time in many years Freddie needed to alter the normal proceedings slightly. He'd promised Lisa he wouldn't drink.

"Just tonic water for me this time please," he said as the waiter ambled away.

He'd never attempted to change anything before as he knew it could potentially upset his uncle's routine, but a promise is a promise, he had no choice.

"She's wants me to be more healthy," he offered by way of an apology. "She thinks it'll give us a better chance of conceiving." He immediately regretted the 'she thinks' bit.

"Really?" Roy was scanning the dim sum, his shiny golden fork raised ready to attack.

"I think you should just be spontaneous and let nature take its course," he said carefully impaling the dumpling closest to him, as he always did.

Freddie tilted his head, laughed and stared quizzically at his uncle.

"What did you just say?"

"What?" Roy demanded.

"Spontaneous! Did you really just tell me to be spontaneous?"

"What?" Roy repeated with a shrug, his mouth now full of food.

The waiter arrived with two large whiskies and

placed them on the table.

"You're a fine one to...excuse me," he called after their server who'd turned his back and was walking away.

"I asked for a tonic."

The waiter took no notice and continued shuffling back to his original position by the pillar.

"Excuse me," Freddie called after him and picked up one of the whiskies and rattled the ice against the glass.

"I asked for a tonic instead of this, can you take..." Before he could finish the sentence the waiter just nodded his head and set off for the bar.

"I think he must be a mate of Steve's, he never waits for the end of a sentence either."

Freddie took a sniff at the single malt but quickly put it down and pushed it towards his table companion before he was tempted.

"Oh just drink it, Lisa will never know." Roy said through another mouth full of food.

"Says the man with absolutely no experience of a women's sixth sense."

Roy picked up his glass and held it aloft. "Here's to my bachelorhood then, and long may it continue."

He held his position and looked at his nephew. "Come on lad, it's a toast, you can't refuse."

Freddie snatched up his glass. "Bachelorhood, and I'll probably be one as well when she finds out about this."

"And how is the delusional Steve these days?" Roy asked when the toast was drunk.

Steve had once begged Roy to be his manager and find him work.

"Desperate for stardom, as ever."

Freddie reached over and picked out a battered king prawn before Roy finished them all.

"Hey!" Roy complained, but was too late to grab it back.

"Within ten minutes of stepping into the theatre every director and producer is subjected to what can only be described as an unmusical barrage of noise."

"I can imagine."

"SAMPs are in this week and he warbled his version of 'This is the Moment' from Jekyll and Hyde at old Stan Banks who promptly said it was the sign he'd been looking for. Next day I hear he's retired, apparently told the committee he'd done all he could for the society and just left."

"Banksy? Retired?" Roy stopped eating, his fork paused somewhere between a prawn dumpling and his mouth.

"Yep, he's not even coming in to see the week out."

"But he's the same age as me and you call him old?"

"You know what his shows are like Uncle. He's produced old shows the old way for years. The average age of the audience so far this week must be sixty plus, and the cast are quite a bit older."

"What are they doing?"

"Oklahoma, but everybody's calling it Oldklahoma."

"What no youngsters at all? How can you put on a show like that without any believable principals? That's just weird."

"Weird is putting it mildly. They're a lovely bunch of people but the performance comes across as a bit peculiar. It feels more like you're spying on the love life of your grandparents rather than seeing wholesome family entertainment."

"Tell me something else Freddie, quickly now before horrendous thoughts about geriatrics in love and having sex burn themselves permanently into my brain," Roy pleaded.

"Well how about this then. The guy playing Curly is coming up from the dressing room on a mobility scooter so as not to overtax himself, and when he sings 'Poor Jud is Dead' no one would be surprised if he was, because the guy playing Jud actually resembles a lifeless corpse, a bit like the show really."

Freddie paused his narrative to grab the last spring roll before it disappeared.

Then he continued. "Since the first performance they've had to shorten 'The Farmer and the Cowman' dance routine because the dancers just couldn't cope. On the first night we even had to put one of them on oxygen."

They were both laughing when the old waiter returned and placed two more large whiskies on the table. As Freddie continued to give his frank analysis of the show, he failed to spot the error.

"The girl playing Ado Annie is excellent though," he added picking up one of the glasses of amber fluid and swirled it around. Without thinking he took a mouthful.

"Hmm that's good," he muttered still oblivious. "You ought to come back with me tonight and take a look at her. Her name's Claire, about my age and way too talented for SAMPs. She'd make a great find for your next production."

He took another guzzle. "Talking of panto, how's

it going?"

Roy had found it almost impossible to find new talent over the past decade, mainly because of all the telly talent shows that had flooded the market. Anyone half decent, or equally half stupid, could be instantly 'spotted' and catapulted to fame without the need of representation. Even after Freddie had left his agency he'd still managed to make decent money, but more recently with potential clients and profits diminishing he'd craved a change of direction and a new challenge, but the performing arts were all he knew.

Then during one of their regular soirees at the Lotus Leaf just a couple of years ago Freddie had suggested that THTC needed to put on a 'bloody good old fashioned laugh a minute pantomime', but none of the local 'Am Dram' companies could be bothered.

That Christmas Roy's newly formed 'Magical Productions' in association with 'The Hidden Theatre Company' had delivered a very successful four week run of Mother Goose to some very enthusiastic audiences.

Roy had found his new project, and pantomime was just the start. The following year a springtime 'musical' production was added to the annual programme and more recently he introduced a regular summer season of murder mystery plays.

"Rehearsals are going really well," Roy said as they finished off the first course. "But we still need a fairy."

The waiter was summoned back again to clear the table and within seconds it had been replenished with another mountain of food.

"You open in four weeks," Freddie exclaimed. "Aren't you cutting things a bit fine?"

"Worry not, I'll find someone, and if all else fails I'll ask my nephew." He started chuckling, "I hear he looks great in sparkly heels, but his wands a bit wonky."

Freddie tried to ignore him, despite the fact he found his uncle very funny.

"So you're not using Adam this year then?" he asked.

"He's still in the production, but after last year's fiasco he's back to playing one of the village henchmen.

"Fiasco? I thought the pink tutu and Doc Martin boots combination was very funny."

"And the beard should have been the clincher. But he played it all too straight and by taking the part seriously he spoilt it."

"Oh be fair Roy, he's spent his life performing Shakespeare. It must really hurt his pride to have to stand there in a pink tutu waving a glittery wand at his age."

"Doublet and hose, tutu and boots, I don't really see any difference. A paying job is food on the table."

Freddie had to agree with that. Roy had always found work for hapless Adam.

"Anyway I definitely think the girl playing Ado Annie is worth a look Uncle."

"Haven't I seen her before?"

"Probably, but until recently she was only a member of the chorus so she's been a bit anonymous until this show."

"Who died?"

They both laughed.

"Okay I'll come and take a look, but keep that mad Fly Captain of yours away from me."

"Oh he's quite harmless really, just a bit enthusiastic."

"And deluded," Roy added with a smile and lifted his glass. "Cheers my boy, God bless us everyone."

"Tiny Tim," Freddie replied raising his glass.

Four

6.50 pm - Freddie was back at the theatre.

After the chaos of the day he'd really enjoyed the meal with his uncle, as he always did. For him there was something inexplicably calming about Roy's unchanging habits, and the time he spent with him each month always left him feeling somehow better about almost everything.

Today had certainly been no different, or maybe it was just the effect brought on by three rather large illicit single malts.

In some ways, Freddie too was as habitually obsessive as Roy, especially when it came to his customary pre-show walk through. It helped him focus on the job in hand, putting all unnecessary thoughts out of his mind, and there were plenty of them milling around inside his head tonight.

His first stop was the cave, the control room at the back of the auditorium where the sound and lighting control equipment is located. It's known as the cave because during a performance it's always dark and full of strange, slightly pungent creatures with rather unpleasant habits.

To keep costs down, most of the amateur societies using the theatre would provide a number of volunteers to help out backstage and front of house, and this often included a couple of excited young 'technicians' to operate the sound and lighting desks in the cave. They were usually sons or boyfriends of the cast, and considered themselves highly qualified to do the job as they either had a GCSE in Drama or had once been a DJ at a mate's party.

In an effort to reduce the risk of costly mishaps between these self proclaimed experts and some very expensive and complex kit, Freddie, Steve or Scotty would usually pre-programme all of the sound and lighting cues for the show during the technical rehearsals, leaving these keen but inexperienced helpers to be told which buttons to press and when.

Even if the arrogant little sods decided they wanted to mess about and add their own touch of artistic interpretation to a show they couldn't, both desks were equipped with electronic locks to prevent anything like that from happening.

Not that that ever stopped them from trying, or spending all week on comms giving their opinions as to how they would make the performance look and sound so much better than it did.

In spite of this the volunteer pair of 'techies' were always tolerated because they had another significant role to play away from the cave, a role they were never told about and yet always carried out happily without even being asked.

To advertise their importance to the show they would often walk around the public areas posing in their obligatory oversized black t-shirts announcing in large ironed-on letters that they were 'Sound Crew' or 'Lighting Crew'. The full time front of house staff were delighted with this situation because by revealing their identity in this way the duo had unwittingly put themselves directly into the firing line if anything ever went wrong. And of course there was always someone complaining that everything was far too loud and 'could they turn it down a bit?'

"You'd best have a word with them about that," the staff would say, pointing them out to any customer having a moan, "I'm sure they'll be delighted to hear your opinion."

When everything had been switched on in the cave and Freddie was happy it was all working as it should be, he grabbed the case of radio microphones and headed for the stage, where Steve and Scotty were making sure the cloths were level and pulled tight on their bars to remove any creases. He checked the props table then opened the secure cupboard and loaded the stage pistol that was being used during the show.

A quick walk around to make sure everything was in place and he called 'Going to Black', the process of turning off all the white lights around the wings and pit area in favour of dark blue ones.

Then he pressed the button to close the main house tabs.

Finally he sat down at the stage control desk, made a phone call to the speaking clock and reset the timers and alarms on the panel in front of him and opened his script at the first cue.

He sat back to survey his domain with a

modicum of pride.

"Time for a coffee please Scotty," he called over to the youngster.

This was his kingdom and Freddie was the king. From his throne he could control and coordinate each element of every performance by making sure everything was in the right place at the right time.

Entertaining the masses was complex and had to be taken seriously, a task Freddie and his crew were very good at.

But the one thing Freddie had absolutely no control over was the delivery of the performance. That was solely in the hands of the actors, led by their director. It's not just a simple matter of speaking the lines and singing the songs, it's about delivering a performance.

So many emotions usually flood the backstage area, and this generates an atmosphere of excitement, creating a 'Buzz' amongst the participants. A good director uses this energy and channels it into the show, bringing a story to life with enthusiasm.

But sadly there had been none of that this week, and specifically no 'Buzz', especially since the director had quit.

Swelford Amateur Musical Players production of Oklahoma was in serious trouble, and it seemed to Freddie that the cast couldn't move on from their director's last minute walk out. Technically his job was done, the show was ready to go, but there was an air of betrayal rather than excitement and the life of the show was slowly draining away. Everything seemed to be going wrong and any enthusiasm they'd once possessed had been replaced by irritation and tension.

They were floundering in a sea of frustration and this was a society in decline. Oklahoma was heading for the rocks.

It was a shame, they were nice people and Freddie felt really sorry for them.

His deliberations carried him back to his own time on stage when, as a young performer, he too had faced an array of extreme emotions. From the sheer joy of performing to the devastation he'd felt when his world had come tumbling down. Many times since then he'd come to realise that never to perform again meant there was little chance he would ever experience the very same exhilaration it used to give him.

As his mind drifted he allowed himself to linger in the past for a moment. It was a period in his life he seldom visited, as the memories were often too painful. He rarely talked about it either and had certainly never revealed his 'artistic' past to anyone here at THTC.

But more recently his uncle's monthly reminder of his 'wasted opportunity' had also prompted recollections of those happy times, which now he was allowing to cheer his mind.

And suddenly, at that very moment, he missed it.

Perhaps his uncle was right, maybe he should at least give it a….

"Is it true Uncle Roy's in tonight?"

Freddie came crashing back to the present.

"Erm yes Steve."

Oh bugger Freddie thought, Roy's going to kill me.

"And no," he added quickly. "And since when did he become your Uncle Roy?"

"Well is he here or not?"

"He came back with me from the Lotus yes, but he's not staying long."

"Where is he now? My whole future rests on finding him before he leaves."

Freddie was imagining a further impromptu tuneless rendition being forced onto yet another defenceless victim. He couldn't let that happen...not to Uncle Roy...he'd promised.

"Look Steve, I know this isn't the nicest thing to hear but maybe you should just accept that if you haven't been signed up as an artiste by now then it's probably not going to happen."

He paused and waited for an angry response.

"Oh I'm sure you're right boss, I've come to that conclusion as well."

That was a surprise.

"My great talent has obviously been overlooked because of a lack of good scouts," Steve continued. "If they can't sing and dance themselves then how can they be expected to know the good from bad? So from now on I'm going to put my gift to good use by passing on information about any good performers we get here. I thought I'd give Uncle Roy first option, for a small consideration of course.

"Oh he'll be thrilled."

"Well of course, and I have my first client in mind."

"Who?"

"Claire, the girl playing Ado Annie, I think she's brilliant."

"Has she agreed to let you represent her yet?"

"Oh I don't want to manage anyone Boss, just pass on the details."

Freddie started laughing.

"Sorry mate, you're too late, Roy's already been tipped off about Claire and that's why he's here."

"Oh bollocks. So who told him then?"

"Well obviously it was me. I've been doing it for years, not that anyone here would know."

"I really thought I was onto a winner then. Oh shit and more bollocks."

"It's a good idea Steve, so I'll do you a deal. If you can persuade 'our' Uncle Roy to give you a finder's fee for future discoveries then I'll butt out."

"Oh cheers Boss."

"But I wouldn't be pushy and demand one for Claire as she's already on his radar. So I suggest you wait to see him till after tonight's show."

"Okay will do."

"Let me speak to him first though," Freddie added quickly knowing what Roy would do if he saw Steve coming towards him.

"Why?"

"I think he's a little bit frightened by your enthusiasm," he said tactfully.

Steve looked thoughtful but seemed happy with the explanation.

"I'll head back up to the fly rail then," he said shaping to leave.

"Oh, just one more thing Boss," he added as if he'd just remembered something. "You were humming or singing something when I came over."

"Was I?" If he was, Freddie didn't remember.

"Yes, and you've been doing quite a lot of daydreaming just lately, accompanied by the humming."

"Have I? I never realised I did that, wow."

67

"Well forgive me for saying so Boss, but I hope you're not fantasising about being out there."

Freddie followed an indicating finger, Steve was pointing to the middle of the stage.

"Well, actually, no."

"That a good job then, because even with years of practice you'll never be as good as me."

Freddie smiled as his colleague walked away.

"Maybe you should mention that to Uncle Roy then. He'll be able to see what a great talent scout you'll make."

Five

11.30 pm - Freddie was home.

As promised he was back earlier than usual and hoping he wasn't going to walk straight into a fight, especially one he knew he couldn't win.

Lisa met him at the front door, and with a big smile she'd kissed him and fussed around helping him out of his coat and hanging it up while he removed his work boots. They walked through to the kitchen where a coffee and sandwich supper was ready for them both.

She often stayed up late if there wasn't an early morning meeting at the magazine, or she just wanted a chance to spend some time with her hard working hubbie.

In all the years they'd been together there had rarely been arguments.

On the day they'd married, when all the pandemonium was over, they'd whispered one simple promise to each other to always be happy together. They both believed this wouldn't be difficult if they were no more demanding of each other than this simple pledge.

So far they'd been right.

She never nagged and he never sulked, mainly because they didn't need to.

He loved to see his beautiful wife content and willingly did everything possible to keep it that way.

She loved the way Freddie always made time to be with her, was exceptionally caring and attentive as well as a great listener who consistently gave good advice, even though sometimes she didn't take it. More importantly they just enjoyed their life together, and of course sex had been the best of the fun.

Any differences had nearly always been resolved with sex.

Lisa knew she couldn't have wished for a better partner and was determined it would always stay that way. She knew exactly what her man wanted and was adamant he'd never have any reason to look elsewhere.

In the early days of the magazine, she had written most of the features and articles herself to keep costs down. But the one role she detested more than anything was playing the part of the Agony Aunt, doling out personal advice for desperate readers begging for someone to make their lives better.

She had little patience and hadn't always been very diplomatic with some of her replies to the disgruntled women who couldn't understand why 'Their Man' had lost interest.

There was little sympathy for their situation and some of her advice had been brutal.

In answer to one she wrote,

'Human desires haven't evolved much for thousands of years so when it comes to sex a modern man is just a Neanderthal wearing trainers and aftershave. If he's looking elsewhere then he's probably searching for the very same thing that attracted him to you in the first place. It doesn't take a genius to work out which one of you has changed.'

Freddie had begged her to employ a more empathetic Advice Columnist.

She'd agreed he may have a point and had been happy to concede on this occasion, but not before she'd advised one concerned parent that it was, 'Perfectly normal for all teenagers to masturbate'.

This of course was absolutely true, but she hadn't left it at that.

'Instead of venting your frustrations by trying to prevent others from pleasuring themselves,' she'd added, 'Maybe it would be better if you bought a vibrator and were a little bit indulgent yourself. Then you'd understand why millions of people do it every day and none of them have gone blind because they did."

Strangely enough, the Agony Aunt's postbag grew considerably during Lisa's 'time in office' despite her 'harsh but honest' guidance.

"Have you had a good day?" he asked her as they sat at the small table in the kitchen laid with a blue and white gingham cloth, complete with a china vase of flowers in the middle.

Lisa seemed back to her usual calm self. Her mood was much better than he was expecting and he quietly reprimanded himself for unfairly prejudging his wife's demeanour.

He would stick it to monkey later as well.

"It's been very busy as usual," she said.

"I went round to Oscar's for the evening to discuss a couple of last minute changes for the March issue. It goes to print over the weekend so I want to get it finalised tomorrow. I only got in about an hour ago."

She drank some coffee but pushed her untouched sandwich away.

"I'm not really hungry to be honest. Oscar ordered pizza and I haven't been to the gym today either."

"I'm still quite full as well," Freddie said.

"I'm sure Roy only eats once a month. The amount of Chinese food he orders would feed an entire family."

"I bet there wasn't much left by the end though."

She stood and picked up her plate and reached for his.

"I'll put these in the fridge then and you can have them for lunch tomorrow."

He fended off her hand and made a grab for the sandwich, squeezing it so hard that some of the filling fell out onto the plate.

"You know me, I just can't resist good food."

He separated the corners of the bread to examine the contents, a little disappointed that Lisa was persisting with chicken and salad on thin sliced wholemeal instead of his favourite cheese and pickle on doorstep white.

"It must be eaten while it's still fresh and I feel compelled to help it achieve its sole purpose for existing."

He took a big bite.

"A happy sandwich is a lingering taste on the

tongue and a few crumbs on the plate."

He was spluttering as he chewed.

"The way you eat the crumbs are nowhere near the plate. Stop it Freddie you're messing up my table cloth."

"Sorry," he said through closed lips.

He swallowed.

"Talking of bad habits, how was your venomous partner in crime?" Freddie asked.

Oscar had been one of the most notable fashion designers of the Glam Rock to New Romantic era of the seventies and eighties. When his outlandish creations were no longer trendy and desirable he'd become one of the industry's most outspoken critics, a role he'd really enjoyed.

When Lisa had first met Oscar she'd made what turned out to be an inspired decision by offering him a job at the magazine, despite the fact she didn't know how she was going to afford to pay him a salary.

Most of the other popular publications had refused to print any of his extremely controversial opinions as they'd wanted to remain popular. But they hadn't realised there was a growing interest among consumers to see confrontational opinions in print.

Lisa had spotted something the big boys had missed.

So with her new partner Oscar, and a generous injection of cash from Freddie, IG Lifestyle quickly became a very successful publication.

"Anyone hearing you call my associate such hurtful things would assume you don't like him very much," Lisa said.

"I only say nasty things to distract you from the fact that I quite fancy him."

He really did like Oscar, and the feeling was mutual. Oscar adored Freddie.

"You wouldn't dare say that to his face," she teased.

"Maybe I should, I hear he's an exceptionally generous lover."

"It's true and he's been without a partner for some time. But I reckon he's fed up not hard up."

She laughed, stood up and kissed the top of Freddie's head.

"Beside he couldn't fancy you, I wouldn't let him. You're all mine."

She picked up the two mugs from off the table.

"Come on," she said brightly, "If you promise not to spit crumbs everywhere you can finish your supper in the living room. We could watch porn and have a chat."

"We never watch porn," he called after her as she disappeared next door.

She popped her head back round the corner.

"Well, at least not together," she said, her smile was enormous.

"Looks like it's just a chat then."

"I don't think I've ever seen anything so funny," Freddie said.

"You know the bit in the second act where Aunt Eller fires a handgun into the air to stop the fight?"

Lisa nodded in agreement.

"Well tonight she couldn't muster enough strength to pull the trigger, so the farmers and cowmen had to keep on wrestling each other."

He chuckled as he recalled the ridiculous events of the evening.

Lisa always showed an interest in his work and especially loved to hear about the things that went wrong, even though sometimes she hadn't any knowledge about the show Freddie was describing.

At least he'd finished eating so the furniture was safe.

"A couple of times the whole cast simultaneously froze in mid punch and went silent for a second or two, trying to see what was happening. Then the brawl would continue as Aunt Eller stomped around the stage desperately trying to fire the gun. In the end I just shouted 'BANG' as loud as possible just to get things going again. If I hadn't well we'd probably all still be there now."

"Sounds as if the show is livening up a bit then."

"You'd think so. But sadly the cast, or more especially Bob the lead, didn't appreciate the laughter coming from the audience, who of course were in stitches by this time. He really tore into me about the whole episode after the show. Stupid git, like it was my fault."

He looked down at his now empty plate.

"Any cakes?"

"I didn't buy any. They're bad for you, too much sugar."

"There's definitely some Jaffa Cakes in the cupboard, I'll just go ..."

"It's so annoying Freddie," she interrupted him. "You're always saying you'll do whatever and yet when I ask you to be a bit more conscientious about your health, you do nothing."

There wasn't any anger in her voice, just a tinge

of concern mixed with a little unhappiness.

"I really don't think I'm overweight or unfit but I have been trying, I even ordered tonic water at the Chinese today."

She wasn't to know that's not what he got.

"I just want you to start looking after yourself properly, it's what's going on inside that can sometimes be the problem. It's not just the baby thing I worry about, I need you to be safe and stay healthy."

She reached over and held his hand.

"Please Freddie."

"I'm sorry, you're right. We young fearless men barge through life thinking we're invincible. I want you to remind me of that from time to time."

"And what else do you want from life my fearless man?"

"You missed out the young bit,"

"I know. It was deliberate."

They were back to laughing again.

"Seriously though."

She looked straight into his eyes. "I know I bulldoze my way through life and I'm sure at some point I've bullied you into doing things you probably haven't wanted to."

"You're wrong. I would gladly do anything just to see you happy. I have no complaints and no regrets."

"And because of that I can never be sure what you really want Freddie. Be honest with me, do you want us to have a baby?"

Freddie sat back and thought for a moment, raised his eyebrows and puckered his mouth, his face displaying an intense look of concentration.

"I can't say I've really given that exact question much consideration at any one particular time. But I've always believed we'd have children, so yes it's what I want."

"Really?"

"I just want us, and us can mean any number of two or more."

"You say the sweetest things."

She snuggled up to his arm.

"But no more than four," he quickly added.

"Right now I'd settle for just three," she said kissing him on the cheek.

"So I've arranged an appointment with Dr Yates, Thursday morning at 10.15am,"

"What? Why?" He pulled his arm away from her. He was sure he'd just been ambushed.

"I've been off the pill for over a year now and nothing is happening in the baby department. If we are to become three we need to find out if everything is working okay."

"It all works fine as far as I'm concerned."

"Well you're definitely doing all the right things in the right place," she giggled. "But so far without success. The doctor will find out if there are any problems."

"But I thought you had to finalise copy tomorrow?"

Lisa hesitated.

"The appointment is for you, not us."

"Oh, so you're automatically assuming it's my fault?"

"It's just easier to get you tested first Freddie" she laughed. "No one is saying it's your fault, but we need to get things checked out."

"By 'we' you mean just me, don't you?"

"I mean 'we' Freddie. But as I said the doctor suggested we start with the easier options, plus we can get some advice about other things we can do to improve our chances."

"By 'we' you're meaning me again. But I really don't see what else we can do."

"How about a healthier diet?"

"Okay, I admit that could improve, but after all those freezing cold baths I need something warm and comforting to cheer me up."

"Like a curry I suppose, what a typical male excuse."

"Treat it as my reward for following every conceivable technique and routine your magazine has ever printed. I'm surprised IGL haven't started an online blog to keep your readership fully informed of the myriad of things we've tried and tested."

"Please Freddie, I love the way you can always make light of any situation but I worry that maybe we've waited too long to start this family. Research says that the further beyond thirty five we go the greater the problems we might encounter."

"And doesn't that include conception? Look sweetie, I don't want to keep quoting 'Lifestyle Hazel' our very own personal sex guru, but even she's suggested it could take up to two years."

"You're right of course, but I still think it's worth seeing the doctor."

"No problem, I'm happy to go if that's what you want, but I'm sure we don't have any problems, it just takes time, trust me."

"Thank you Freddie," she hugged his arm again,

kissed him and got to her feet, "I really appreciate that and I'm sure you're probably right."

Collecting the mugs and plates she disappeared into the kitchen.

"Talking of time," Freddie said stretching his arms. "It's well past two and we've got to suffer another day of Neil's idiotic antics. I should get to bed, but I'm just going to jump in the shower first," he called out in her general direction.

He started to dutifully plump the cushions.

"I'll join you in the shower if you fancy."

The lovely Lisa was standing in the doorway, one hand on her waist the other on the doorframe, a very cheeky grin on her lips.

"Now that's what I really want. My lovely lady in the shower, naked. Hang on a mo though, I didn't think we would tonight, not while..."

"Doesn't stop us from having a bit of fun, unless you're not interested."

"You bet I am, but I hope this isn't a bribe to make sure I keep that appointment with the doctor."

"Certainly not. It's more a reward for your new idea for IGL."

"What Idea? I don't remember any new idea."

"The one about publishing a blog, I really like it. I'll get the features department working on it straight away."

Six

Wednesday 27th 2.05 pm - The final day of the first aid course wasn't going well.

At first it seemed that Neil the trainer had finally accepted this group didn't want to be entertained and he'd started the morning session in the same subdued manner of the previous afternoon. Freddie had been really happy with the way things were progressing, but it wouldn't be long before Neil rekindled his determination to prove how funny he considered himself.

By twelve thirty everyone had been bored to death by his never ending 'something funny happened' stories and tempers had started to fray, especially Steve's. So Freddie had called an early lunch to prevent a riot.

"You really must stop this nonsense," he'd told Neil once the rest of the staff had left the stage.

"I wish you'd all lighten up Freddie and have a bit of fun occasionally," was the defiant response.

"We always have fun chap and we love funny,

but sadly you're not, so stop trying to be."

"I think…"

"Then please don't," Freddie had interrupted, "Just finish the job without the jokes and then you can leave us to wallow in our own miserable, unfunny world, okay."

As before, he hadn't waited for a reply, he didn't want one.

As he'd approached the green room Freddie had heard excited chatter and laughter coming from the other side of the door.

"See," he'd announced to no one in particular, "We have fun all the time."

But as soon as he'd entered the room everything had suddenly gone quiet.

"What's going on?" he'd asked suspiciously as Steve, Scotty, Brian, Ann and Amy stood staring guiltily at the floor.

They'd all muttered their innocence as one, "Oh…erm…nothing Boss…just saying…erm the food's been good…erm…have a crisp."

"I hope you're not planning anything untoward for the hapless git next door."

"Oh no Boss, never crossed our minds. Why would you think such a thing?"

"Good, then let's eat and get this fiasco finished."

With lunch over and Neil waiting to begin, the staff trudged back to the stage, and as they took their seats Freddie couldn't help but notice the looks they were exchanging with each other.

Neil began.

"We've got about an hour before the assessment which we're going to use to recap and practice the recovery position. Scotty, you're going to be the casualty for this exercise so come and lie on the floor over here, please."

At nineteen Scotty was the youngest and probably the fittest of the back stage crew, so whenever Neil had called for a volunteer during the course he'd accepted that the look from Freddie meant 'That'll be you then lad' and so he'd acted as the casualty for nearly all the practical demonstrations so far.

After three long days poor Scotty was fed up.

"Maybe it could be someone else's turn to volunteer this time?" he asked in Freddie's direction. "This floor is really hard and uncomfortable."

"I'll put a couple of blankets down for you then," Neil said quickly. "Come on, hurry up. Your boss wants me to speed things along."

Reluctantly Scotty got to his feet, shuffled to where Neil had quickly laid out the blankets and with a big sigh flopped down, back to the floor, arms by his side, feet together and head straight with his nose pointing at the ceiling. He blew out his cheeks and shut his eyes.

Neil continued, "As you can see folks, Scotty has adopted the British Standard mortuary position."

He paused for effect, but there was no reaction. "So if you ever find someone like this they're not really a casualty, they're either asleep or dead."

Steve groaned loudly.

"That was funny the first time on the first day mate, and mildly amusing the other fifty times, but not today."

Neil ignored him, "Now we need to help Scotty."

"Why?" Steve shouted. "After all if he's only

asleep or dead he just needs a pillow or an undertaker."

Everyone except Neil and Freddie laughed.

"Okay okay, it wasn't that funny, let's move on. I want you to imagine you've just walked into Scotty's office and found him collapsed on the floor. Thinking of the procedures we've covered on the course, what's the first thing you're going to do?"

"Nick his wallet," shouted Steve. More laughter erupted.

Fly captain Steve was a nice guy who worked hard and consistently did his job well. But he was also a bit of a joker and always playing pranks on the cast and crew. He'd been particularly keen to attend this course and had given assurances that he would temper his antics and take it seriously, so the boss had said okay.

But now Freddie was wondering if Steve was getting a bit too vocal and forgetting his promise? Maybe he should stop this banter.

'Oh sod it' he thought, 'let's see where this is going'.

Neil's squeaky voice disturbed his deliberations. "This is important Steve and could save someone's life one day, just stop mucking about okay."

"Sorry mate," Steve said, "You're right, I really should think before I speak."

Freddie looked up. Had he just heard an apology from Steve?

Neil too was momentarily lost for words. The others stopped fidgeting or doodling and were all now staring directly at Steve, who was sheepishly looking straight down at the floor, his body language suggesting he was feeling embarrassed. For what seemed an age the room was totally still.

Neil broke the silence, "Okay, apology accepted."

The trainer's face was showing a broad smile which was about to disappear.

"Yes I'm sorry because I realise I should have made sure nobody was watching first, then nick his wallet."

"No no no Steve," Neil shrieked. "You need to look for dangers."

"In that case I'd carefully look around for the bloke who'd bashed him, and then it'd be safe to nick his wallet."

"This really is not helping Steve, and you're just wasting time," Neil exclaimed.

"But I think he has a point," said Brian.

"What? He doesn't have a point Brian. He's just trying to be the centre of attention, again. Can we move on please?"

"Well," said Brian, obviously not ready to move on and wanting to have his say.

"It's quite possible that Scotty has been violently assaulted, his wallet stolen and the perpetrator is now lurking in the darkness waiting to pounce on his next victim. Surely that's a danger?"

The others started to mutter their support of this clever observation.

"Okay that's possible I suppose," Neil reluctantly agreed. "But..."

Brian was far from finished.

"My friend got attacked back in March last year and ended up in hospital. The police never found the person that did it."

"Maybe it's the same guy who's attacked Scotty and now he's lurking in the dark, waiting to pounce on his next victim," offered Steve.

"Do you think so? Oh God I hope not." Brian lifted his hands to his face and covered his eyes. "I couldn't go through all that again."

Neil's jaw dropped in disbelief, trying to comprehend how this ridiculous drama had started.

"My husband had his phone stolen by a Goth on a skate board." Ann from the front office joined in. "He said it was like being attacked by a ninja assassin. Never saw him, never heard him."

"I'm confused Ann, was it a ninja assassin or a Goth?"

"Oh definitely a Goth, but he moved like a ninja assassin. He only stole his phone, but it probably wasn't worth killing him for his old Nokia."

It sounded like Brian had started to whimper.

"But how did he know it was a Goth if he never saw him?"

"Oh he saw him running away, well skate boarding, just never saw him coming and the police never found him either."

Freddie hadn't changed his expression or made eye contact with anyone, he had an inkling of what was going on and wasn't going to intervene, yet.

"Well then it's obvious my dear Watson."

Steve stood and lifted his hand to smoke an imaginary pipe. "The person responsible for beating Scotty and nicking his wallet is the very same person who attacked Brian's friend and stole Ann's husband's phone. Ladies and Gentleman the perpetrator is none other than a Goth on a skateboard who is now lurking in the darkness of Scotty's office."

Brian gasped, Ann squealed, Freddie's body

started shaking as he tried desperately not to laugh out loud. Neil, who hadn't a clue what was going on, had sat down on the floor by Scotty, who sounded like he was quietly snoring.

"The only problem folks is we'll never know who he is," Steve continued and dramatically placed a hand on Brian's' shoulder.

"Well you could never find a Goth if he's lurking in the darkness."

Like a greyhound out of the trap Brian was up and running for the door.

"I'm phoning the police before the bastard has chance to escape, I bet he knows we're on to him."

"Brian, Brian hang on a minute," called Freddie realising that maybe this had gone far enough now.

"Come and sit down a minute while we think about this rationally."

He took a hankie out of his pocket, wiped his eyes and took a deep breath.

"Can we assume that a Goth on a skateboard in a theatre is a little out of place and would have been noticed. Besides which, without a ticket security wouldn't let him past the foyer." He was still trying not to laugh as he spoke, but was failing miserably.

"That's a shame, I think we should have handed him over to the police," said Brian returning to his seat. "At least they could question him about the assault on my friend and Ann's husband."

"I'll ask security to be vigilant, but for now maybe we should let Neil finish this practice session. Neil, can we assume that there are no dangers?" Freddie looked over at Steve and caught his eye hoping that he would understand the 'that was funny but no more interruptions please' look.

"Okay, so there are NO obvious signs of danger." Neil continued with a scowl aimed at Steve, it was time to prove he was smarter and certainly a lot funnier.

"So next we need a...?" he asked.

"A response," the group said in unison.

"Okay then. Steve come and see if you can get a response out of Scotty. How about it funny man, think you can remember what to do?"

Steve didn't get the chance to react, instead young Amy got to her feet like a rocket.

"I really think it's my turn," she said and walked toward Scotty.

Neil's expression suggested this was the last thing he'd expected or wanted. "No, Steve thinks he knows it all, he has to do it." He moved to block her path but she nudged him aside.

"Nobody ever asks me to do anything and I want a go, it'll be fun," she insisted.

Steve didn't appear to be very happy about this either, he was up on his feet as well and his mood had suddenly changed.

"You're not doing it," he sounded almost angry. "You're not here to have fun, and certainly not with Scotty," he said waving his arms around in apparent annoyance.

Pretty nineteen year old Amy was part of the front of house team, and had only been working at the theatre for a short while. When Brian had first introduced her to Freddie and the stage crew she'd appeared to be a very shy and nervous individual, and hadn't really joined in the conversations much during the breaks.

But now she'd found her voice at last.

"Since when do you get to tell me what to do?" she demanded. "So you can sit down Steve because I'm going to help Scotty."

"Yes, sit down Steve," Freddie barked, confused as to what was really going on here. Had he missed something?

Amy was now standing by the side of recumbent Scotty who opened an eye and smiled up at her and she smiled back.

"Okay then Amy you're the first aider," Neil said. "So you're going to show us the right way to try and get a response from the casualty."

Amy followed the techniques Neil had explained to them the day before.

"Scotty? Scotty can you hear me?" she called softly, "Can you open your eyes for me?"

Scotty's eyes remained tightly shut.

Amy knelt down by the side of him and gently tapped him on the shoulder, "Scotty, open your eyes."

"Did you get any response Amy?" Neil asked.

She shook her head, "No."

"Does turning a bright shade of pink constitute a response?" Ann said with a giggle.

Freddie was aware that Neil was watching Steve, but why? He also noticed Steve was scowling at Amy and Scotty. There was definitely something going on, but what?

"Let's assume for now," Neil said, "That Amy got NO response from Scotty, and there are just the two of them in the office, what should she do now?"

"Call for help," said Brian and Ann in unison.

"Okay," said Neil, moving to stand behind Amy. "So she shouts for help and through the office window she can see the cleaner hurrying to help." He reached down and gently touched her shoulder, "And I'm here as well if you need anything."

Amy didn't appreciate this uninvited contact and quickly dipped her shoulder to get away from Neil's hand.

"So next I need to open his airway and check his breathing like we practiced yesterday," she said.

"Good, show us how you will do that please Amy, and let's hope you find he's still breathing."

"Oh yeah, let's," muttered Steve.

Amy placed two fingers under Scotty's chin and carefully lifted it forward which tilted his head back.

"Good, so that opens the airway," Neil said. "Now you need to check he's using it. Put your ear close to his mouth and look down towards his feet, that way you can listen for breathing sounds, feel for breath on your face and look to see if the chest is rising and falling."

"I can see he's breathing from over here," shouted Steve.

"We all know this is just pretend Steve," Brian said helpfully. "But she still needs to check properly though."

"But she doesn't need to get too close," Steve added quickly.

"No, I'll do it properly," Amy insisted. "We'll have to do it correctly later so might as well have a proper practice."

"Quite right," Neil added with a smile in Steve's direction. "And don't forget Amy, as I told you yesterday, if the casualty is breathing it would probably be very shallow so you need to be as close as you can get, so close that if they were to stick out their tongue it would go straight in your ear. Do you remember that bit Steve?"

"Let's assume she's checked and he's breathing." Steve's voice had definitely gone up a few tones and he was starting to gabble. "We all know he's breathing so stop wasting time, what's next?"

"Like I said, I want to do it properly," Amy said.

Not waiting for approval she repositioned herself to check Scotty's breathing. As she bent lower to get closer her long blonde hair slid off her opposite shoulder and cascaded across Scotty's face.

Steve jumped up. "That's not very good at all, a casualty doesn't want a face full of your hair, get up Amy I'll take over."

"He's unconscious isn't he?" Amy shouted back and sat upright. "So why would it matter?"

Steve didn't have an answer and sat down again.

"Right, I'll do it again then, how long should I check for?"

"Ten seconds," called Ann.

Amy retook the correct position and quietly counted to ten as the others watched on. Steve was tutting loudly but said nothing.

"Eight, nine, ten. He's breathing," she said sitting upright.

"So he's unconscious but still breathing. With that information the office cleaner has been sent off to call for an ambulance. Whilst waiting for the paramedics to arrive what else does she need to do?"

"Put him in the recovery position to protect his airway," shouted Ann.

"Good thinking Ann, but before she does that could there be any other problems that would cause Scotty's condition to deteriorate, if left undetected and treated?"

The room went silent so Neil continued.

"In our ABC of first aid, Amy so far has opened his A, Airway and checked his B, Breathing. He is breathing so we know his heart is beating but what could be happening to his C, Circulation that could be a major problem if left unchecked?"

"He's probably bleeding from an injury caused by that bloody Goth," Brian called. There was still a lot anger in his voice as he spoke.

"Scotty's fine Brian, don't worry," Ann reached over and patted his hand.

"I still can't believe he's going to get away with it, again, I'm furious about the whole bloody situation."

"That's right Brian," Neil confirmed. "He could be losing a lot of blood from an injury somewhere."

Amy sat up and looked straight at Steve.

"So I need to do a thorough check of Scotty to ensure he's not losing any blood, don't I Neil? And the best way to do this is for me to put on a pair of disposable gloves and have a good grope, isn't it Neil? oops sorry, I mean carefully feel down his body checking for injuries."

Steve was on his feet again.

"Oh come on," he called, "If there was blood you'd see it, no need to go groping."

"Maybe," said Neil. "But blood could be gathering between him and the floor and not yet visible. He's wearing dark coloured clothing so even if you could see a damp patch you wouldn't be able to tell whether it was blood or maybe just a cup of coffee he threw down himself as he collapsed. So Amy's right, she needs to run her hands around and feel under the hollows and down his limbs to see if

Scotty has any other problems and is losing blood."

"He'll have a problem soon enough." Steve muttered as he sat back down.

Using both of her hands Amy started to carefully feel over the top of Scotty's head then moved down to check under his neck and shoulders.

"So after the head and shoulders, carefully check down each of his arms, any swelling or deformity could signify an injury."

Amy was following Neil's instructions very methodically.

"There's one other very important thing to know." Neil was saying, "It is thought that an unconscious casualty can possibly still hear and be aware of what is going on around them, so it would be a good idea to tell them that you're feeling for injuries and not just having a good grope."

Amy had just finished a careful investigation under the hollow of his back, and she was taking Neil's advice.

"I'm just going to check down your legs for any injuries Scotty."

Amy reached his feet and announced she had found no injuries.

"So now Scotty should be put into the recovery position while we wait for the ambulance," Neil said. "But there are a couple of important things we need to do to ensure we turn him over safely. Firstly, while we're by his feet we need to straighten his legs if necessary, and make sure his heels are together."

Amy followed the instructions.

"Next, we need to remove anything bulky from his pocket that might hurt him as we roll him over, such as a bunch of keys or his mobile phone. Amy just check the pocket nearest to you by patting around it with the back of your hand."

"There's nothing in my pocket," Scotty said quickly. He suddenly seemed in a bit of a panic.

"You're supposed to be unconscious mate, Amy needs to make sure."

Amy had moved from his feet and was kneeling by his side, looking down at the pocket in his jeans nearest to her and gently exploring it with the back of hand.

"There really is nothing in that pocket," Scotty pleaded.

"Yes there is, I can feel it."

"Trust me it's nothing."

"I can see it as well, there look. I'll get it out."

Amy pushed her hand deep into Scotty's pocket. "I can feel it, but can't grab hold of it. It's not in his pocket it's growing...oh my god," she squealed.

Everyone in the room suddenly realised what she was referring to.

Steve leapt to his feet and rushed at Scotty, quickly sidestepping to avoid Neil in the process. "You horny little shit, you're going to get it now," he yelled.

Scotty had just about managed to get to his knees by the time Steve reached him, but Neil could see there was no escape for the youngster. To his horror he saw Steve's right arm pull back in a big arc and plunge towards Scotty, there was a sickening smack and Scotty fell forward, his hands clutching at his face.

Everyone started screaming.

Amy was screaming.

Brian and Ann were screaming.

Scotty with his hands cupped over his face was screaming. "You've broke my nose you bastard, what was that for?"

"You know why you little shit."

Neil just stood there flabbergasted.

"Are you completely mad Steve....you psycho?" he yelled. He spun round to confront Freddie.

"Why didn't you stop him? You people are all nuts. I can't believe you just let him..."

Neil suddenly realised that the only one not reacting was Freddie. He was still sitting with his legs crossed and arms folded, a slight grin showing on his lips.

Now Neil was screaming.

"Your staff are fighting Freddie and you just sit there, DO SOMETHING."

"You're absolutely right chap, I should."

Freddie slowly stood and to Neil's amazement started to clap. "I don't think anymore first aid practice is going to help us folks, time for another cuppa I reckon," he said. "That was one hell of a deserving performance, don't you think Neil?"

"WHAT?" Neil shrieked.

"Maybe next time you shouldn't try to outwit a group of professional wits."

All the commotion had suddenly stopped and the screaming had turned to laughter. Neil looked round at the group in disbelief.

Ann and Brian were walking off to the green room arm in arm to put the kettle on and the other three youngsters were excitedly hugging and patting each other's backs, all their anger and aggression gone.

There wasn't a single mark to be seen on Scotty's

face and as Freddie joined his colleagues Neil would have heard him say, "Was everyone in on that?"

"Of course Boss," said Steve. "But the only thing we had in mind was the fight between me and Scotty, how we got there and everything else was all impromptu."

Steve was obviously buzzing.

"You guys are pros, how do you do it?" Amy said looking straight at the still pink eared Scotty.

"Steve's been teaching me how to take a stage punch," Scotty said.

"Well it fooled me. It was brilliant, if not a little too realistic."

"You're one to talk." Freddie patted Amy's back.

"Well done you as well, we all thought you were little Miss Innocent until now. What a great imagination you have, making up the 'growing thing' in Scotty's pocket."

Scotty was glowing bright red now.

Amy giggled. "Oh I didn't make that bit up."

Seven

Thursday 28th 10.22 am - Freddie raised his hand and made a loose fist, but as his eyes focused on the door in front of him something he saw made him hesitate.

As an adult he'd never needed to consult a doctor for any reason and he certainly didn't want to be here now. He felt like a fraud, a time waster abusing an already overstretched service, but more than anything else there was the embarrassment. It was welling up inside him right now, making him feel uncomfortable with the thought of what he was about to discuss with a complete stranger.

But a promise is a promise, so before he had time to make a million more excuses he squared his shoulders and knocked on the door, right next to the over polished brass plaque announcing this was the consulting room of Dr Danielle Yates MBBS MRCP.

Lisa had failed to mention the appointment was with a lady doctor, which certainly didn't help as far as Freddie was concerned.

A bright chirpy voiced called from within, "Come in please."

With a growing knot in the pit of his stomach he pushed the door open and stepped into the room. Behind a very large untidy desk, and partially hidden from view by a huge flat screen monitor, the occupant was busily tapping away at a keyboard.

"Good morning Mr Hobbs," the desk dweller said without looking up. "Take a seat, I won't keep you a moment."

Freddie grunted some sort of acknowledgement and moved toward the chair by the side of the desk. Then just as he was about to park his bum on the seat a face peeked around the side of the monitor and smiled, it was a face he instantly recognised.

"Freddie, how lovely it is to see you again."

"Danni...what are you doing here?" he blurted out, now feeling even more flustered and very confused.

"Well I'm fairly sure that's my name on the door, but I can go and check if you like," she chuckled. "Or maybe it's not really me and I'm actually somebody else I never knew about."

Although he hadn't seen her for ages, this strikingly beautiful and intelligent lady was exceptionally well known to him, or at least he'd thought so. For a number of years she'd been a member of one of the local am dram groups and had appeared in several musical productions on his stage at THTC. Then as a distraction during her rather unpleasant divorce she'd spent a lot of her spare time helping out backstage as one of the volunteer crew members.

Throughout her ordeal the two of them had often

sat drinking wine in the green room late into the night. As usual Freddie had been very supportive and encouraging, lending a shoulder to cry on and an ear for her to vent her anger about her husband's infidelity. He'd spent many hours helping her to realise that she wasn't to blame and that given time her life would be wonderful again.

They had become quite good friends, but apart from her turbulent relationship issues Danni's private life had remained mainly unspecified and right at this moment Freddie was starting to realise that he didn't know her quite as well as he'd considered.

"I thought your name was Moore, and you never told me you were a doctor."

Freddie settled himself down in the chair.

"Yates is my maiden name Freddie, I changed it back after the divorce. I buried the demons and made a fresh start, just like you told me to, remember?"

"Not really, that sounds far too profound for me. I must try harder to be a bit more flippant or I'll completely ruin my image." They both laughed. "So how are you keeping?"

"I'm really good thanks. It took a while to completely rid myself of that idiot husband of mine, but it's all been worth it."

"Glad to hear it. We've really missed you at the theatre, enthusiastic volunteers like you are becoming hard to find."

"It was great fun and I've often considered coming back to help. But just lately things are so hectic I just like to relax when I get home in the evenings, with a nice glass of wine."

"Or three I reckon," he teased. "You should at

least come along for the opening night party on the twenty third. Roy's lot are doing Cinderella this year and the cast and crew are having a bit of a do after press night. It's always a good laugh and everyone would love to see you again."

"Except King Rat maybe."

"Oh yes, I remember that. You coated the inside of his false nose with the contents of a stink bomb, all because he'd refused to stop calling you darling."

"He got quite upset about it as I remember, but he was so obnoxious."

"Upset? He was furious. But Sanjay the director was elated, said it stimulated the talentless rodent into giving his best performance of the run and could we upset him every night? I seem to remember you made it your personal responsibility to do exactly that."

"And I enjoyed every minute of it."

They both laughed at the memory.

"Don't worry," Freddie said, "Ratty's not in this year's panto so please say you'll come along. Anytime after ten, unless of course you fancy a bit of volunteering again."

"I wish I could as I don't have much of social life nowadays if I'm honest. But I only have clinics here until seven so I'm usually free for the rest of the evening. I'll come along if I don't fall asleep in front of the telly."

"That would be great. Now I'm really glad that I came to see you today."

"Talking of which," Danni said, "As nice as it is to reminisce with you my old friend, I have a full waiting room and need to press on, sorry. How can I help?"

Freddie paused for a second or two then started to stand up.

"I'm sorry too Danni, it's really great to meet up again but I'm not sure I want to discuss my problem with someone I know, it would be embarrassing enough telling a stranger. I think I'll make another appointment with one of the other doctors."

"Come on Freddie, please sit down. Just call me Dr Yates and try to forget you know me. I've already had a chat with Mrs Hobbs on the phone so there are no secrets and I'm aware of her concerns. You're trying for a baby, yes?"

Again Freddie paused for a second or two and then retook his seat.

"Yes we are, Dr Yates."

"You can trust me to help if I can Freddie."

"I'm not sure there's a problem doc apart from the fact my wife can be a little impatient."

"Rude to ask I know, but how old are you both?"

"We're both thirty seven, well at least I will be in a couple of weeks."

"And how long have you been trying?"

"Just about a year now, but from what I've heard that's not a long time."

"It isn't really, but then sometimes the harder we try the less we succeed. How often do you have intercourse?"

Freddie shifted uncomfortably in his seat.

"Erm, mostly it's every day, but usually at different times to fit in around work schedules."

"It doesn't have to be that often if finding time is a problem. It's considered that intercourse every two to three days is usually sufficient and probably better."

"She insists we have sex every day because of an Australian study she'd read. It suggested that regular ejaculations empty out weak and damaged sperm allowing strong healthy little swimmers to develop."

"It's one good theory amongst many, but every day is probably not really necessary."

"Maybe not, but to be honest I'm really not going to complain. I'm not ashamed to admit that even after many years I still really enjoy sex with my wife. So I'm okay with the everyday bit unless you think it poses a problem."

He felt he was starting to relax a bit more.

"Not at all, it's all down to personal choice, and of course ability."

She paused, giving her witty friend an opportunity to give some kind of comical response, but Freddie actually appeared to be taking this seriously for the moment.

"But I will say," Danni continued, amazed by a lack of boastful comments, "As sperm count is usually at its highest in the morning it would probably be a good idea if you concentrated on having intercourse then to maximise your chances."

"I can't say I'd be too keen on that, but if it helps then I'll tell her."

"Great, it could make a difference. So what else have you been doing?"

"We've been following all the usual tried and tested advice given by the expert magazine gurus and she's always keen to try different ideas she's read about."

"Lisa reads a lot by the sound of it."

"To be fair it's her job, as is putting me through the torture of cold baths, loose underwear and high fibre diets. Three items that definitely never made it onto Julie Andrews list of favourite things. But then neither did men, sex or chocolate so go figure."

Dr Yates ignored him or was at least trying to, but was failing miserably.

"Back to being a little more serious please Mr Hobbs," she sniggered.

"Sorry," he said, thinking this wasn't turning out too bad after all.

"What about your lifestyle, do you smoke or drink?"

"I've never smoked and just lately I rarely drink, it's not allowed."

"Define rarely."

"Less than not often enough."

"Are you being honest with me Freddie, you used to enjoy a drink, or four?"

"Totally honest doc, Lisa keeps telling me that telling lies causes impotency."

"And where did she read that little gem?"

"I'm pretty sure she probably wrote that one herself."

Dr Yates was starting to wish that all her patients would be this entertaining, but sadly most of them had undergone a humourectomy, without anaesthesia.

"And she's been to the health food shop and bought a load of complementary preparations she's insisting I take," Freddie continued, "Apparently it's a regime designed to help my sperm be a bit more motivated."

"Like what?"

"She's got me on supplements of iron, zinc, copper, chromium, selenium and magnesium, I'm not quite sure if we're trying to make a baby or build a robot."

Now the doctor was in fits of laughter.

Freddie loved an appreciative audience so he added, "I'm supposed to be avoiding xenoestrogens but I haven't got a damn clue who they are or what they look like. I'm not even allowed to use the toilet paper at work, which when you consider the high fibre diet, could be disastrous."

"Stop Freddie, please stop. I have to see some seriously ill patients later on today and I can't be sniggering away thinking about this consultation."

"So what's the plan doc?"

Danni took a hand full of tissues from the box on her desk, wiped her eyes and tried to recompose herself.

"It is certainly true that at the age you are fertility does decline, for both parties, but I'm sure you're both doing the right things to increase the chance of conceiving. I certainly don't think I can add anything at this point, at least not until I have spoken with your wife again. Roll up a sleeve please Mr Hobbs."

While Freddie took of his jacket and unbuttoned a cuff Dr Yates stood up from her desk and walked over to a small metal trolley which she wheeled over to the desk, took out a pair of surgical gloves from a dispenser on the wall and put them on as she spoke.

"I agree with you that generally it's still early days. Considering you're both in your late thirties I can also accept Lisa's desire for things to move on as quickly as possible. I'd like to do a blood test and I'll need a semen sample for a sperm count."

"What now?"

"Yes to the blood, I'll do that now, but no to the

semen, you'll need to collect a sample pot from reception and before you ask, take it home to fill it please."

She unsheathed the blood collecting needle and placed it against his arm.

"Sharp scratch Mr Hobbs."

"Is that the same as tiny prick Dr Yates?"

"Oh no, I'm intending this to hurt a lot more than that."

10.42 am - The telephone was ringing and Freddie was dying inside.

"Sorry Mr Hobbs, could you repeat that please?"

The 8mm sheet of safety glass installed to protect the doctor's receptionist from angry and frustrated patients did very little to preserve patient confidentiality.

"I need a sample pot," Freddie repeated a little louder.

The surgery was packed and so he was trying desperately hard to be heard by just one pair of ears.

"Excuse me?" she still hadn't heard his request.

Freddie winced.

Fifteen minutes earlier when he'd been sitting in the waiting area, just a few feet away from the spot he was now occupying, he'd witnessed a public flogging of human dignity. A well dressed but frail looking older man had been standing at the glass screen. "The doctor has written you a prescription for incontinence pants Mr Harris," the receptionist hollered as if she'd been trying to address anyone named Harris within screaming distance. "And if you need more pads you'll need to contact the District Nurses, okay?"

Mr Harris had shrugged and shuffled out of the surgery door, his head and shoulders slumped in humiliation, an indignant look on his face.

Freddie was determined not to be another victim, but this wasn't going well.

"I just need a sample pot, please." Freddie repeated a third time but now quite a bit louder.

"So you need a sample pot?"

"Yes, please!"

"What for?" the receptionist asked.

"Because the doctor wants me to provide a sample."

"Well yes I realise that, but what type of sample pot?"

"Just a sample pot." Freddie hesitated, "Erm, a small one?" he added hoping that was sufficient information. He immediately crossed his fingers in his pocket as the telephone continued with its desperate quest to be attended to. Its harshness was ringing in his ears along with the pounding pulse of his embarrassment.

The receptionist set her face to impatient mode and her voice increased in volume jarring his brain even further. She needed more information.

"Is it for urine, faeces, nails, phlegm or semen?"

Freddie instantly saw a glimmer of hope and quickly lunged for it. "The last one," he squeaked, but even as the words left his mouth the receptionist held up her hand.

"Just one moment please." She reached across the counter and snatched up the receiver. The persistence of the caller had finally paid off, but at what price?

"Swelford Surgery," she shrieked. "Hold the

line." She banged the phone down on the counter, pressed the hold button on the base and turned back to face Freddie.

"So which pot did you need then Mr Hobbs?"

"The last one," Freddie repeated.

"Which was that then?"

Freddie had wondered why she'd chosen that very moment to answer the phone and now he knew. She was playing him and he didn't stand a chance. She was totally in charge of this situation and like the proverbial 'dog with the rabbit' she wasn't going to let go.

He realised that his name might just as well be Mr Harris and the best chance he had to protect what was left of his dignity was just to say the word and move on.

To his amazement the receptionist, who hadn't taken her eyes off him for a second, raised one eyebrow and nodded.

"Semen," he muttered incredulously.

"Sorry?" an exaggerated lean forward, "Didn't catch that."

Freddie was starting to understand why there was a need for the protective barrier.

"Semen," he shouted.

Her face softened and a smile appeared at the corner of her mouth. She was obviously content.

"Give me a moment please." She disappeared into a side cupboard.

Standing there facing the glass Freddie swore he could hear giggling behind him. But he remained stiff legged, head held high and looking at the reflection of the seven people sitting behind him. He could see every last one of them reflected in the glass, staring at the back of his head. They weren't even pretending to read the tatty magazines they were holding. He wanted to turn round and glare back, make them look away, who knows he may cause one of them to move suddenly and strain a muscle.

But he didn't, instead he stood patiently and waited despite the turmoil in his head. Everyone now knew his reason for being there, and thanks to 'her' his very manhood was under scrutiny.

"There you go Mr Hobbs," the receptionist had returned from her cupboard and handed a small plastic pot and card through the letterbox hole in the bottom of the screen.

"It needs to be a fresh sample and taken to the clinic within an hour of collection, the address is on the card." She sounded really bright and chirpy. "So don't leave them to die on your bedside table overnight."

Freddie grabbed the pot and was off like a rocket, the quicker he got out the better. But just as he reached the door that loud chirpy voice came at him again like a black mood you just can't shake off.

"And don't use a condom to collect the sample Mr Hobbs," it yelled.

11.05 am - He phoned Lisa as soon as he got back home from the surgery.

"What a morning of humiliation I've had to go through," he said when she answered.

"Sorry sweetie but can we discuss this later? I'm rather tied up at the moment."

"Okay, but I just wanted to let you know the doctor thinks we're doing all of the right things in the right way for the best chance, we just need to be patient."

"Good to know, but..."

"And I've been given a plastic pot into which I need to deposit an intimate sample. I was rather hoping you could lend a hand, or two later."

"When I'm with you Freddie I'm not going to waste an opportunity to conceive. You need to sort 'this sample' out yourself."

"Surely you can't imagine I'd find this lump of plastic desirable, I need my incredibly sexy wife to get me going, and coming."

"That's not going to happen Freddie, and you need to do it now so you've recovered for when I get home tonight."

"Okay, how about a bit of phone sex then? Help me out here, it'll be fun."

"When I'm pregnant we can go back to having fun, but until then you and the pot are on your own...and on conference call by the way."

"Hello Freddie darling." It was Oscar.

"I'll come round if you like, or I can call you later if you prefer."

Eight

6.00 pm - Freddie had been at the theatre all afternoon.

After the phone call to Lisa he'd decided he might as well get into work before lunch. There was no particular purpose for the early start but he was confident he'd find something that needed his urgent attention, after all he had nothing better to do at home, or at least nothing he fancied doing alone.

When he got there Ann and Amy were busy in the small back office trying to sort out THTC's 'What's on Guide'. But his offer of help was quickly dismissed, because when it came to paperwork Freddie was prone to be an ass rather than an asset. So before he could meddle with anything Ann had ushered him out from under their feet.

"If you want to be useful then make us all a coffee," she said as she physically nudged him towards the door.

"Then take the staff files and make sure everyone's training records are up to date."

She made a mental note to remind Amy to check them thoroughly when they came back, if they ever did.

After drinks Freddie had set about his assigned task with his usual muted enthusiasm. He'd collected the personnel files and laid them out neatly on a makeshift desk in the green room, as he'd been banned from the office, then toddled off to fetch one of the comfy high backed chairs from the cave.

With another fresh steaming mug of coffee in hand everything was finally in place so he took his seat, plonked his feet firmly on the desk and selected the first folder from the pile, his own.

He stared at the cover blankly for a few minutes pondering his next move which didn't take long to decide. Placing the unopened file down on his outstretched legs he folded his arms and closed his eyes. He allowed his mind to meander through the events of his extraordinarily funny day so far.

Now this was something he was really good at.

Between short naps, as the hours passed unnoticed, he'd replayed the mornings encounter with his old friend doctor Danni and her rottweiler receptionist, and for the umpteenth time the memory had put a stupidly enormous grin on his face.

Just then Brian walked in with another brew and a huge slice of lemon drizzle cake.

"You look like a naughty school boy having a wet dream," he called out.

"I can honestly say it's been a very long time since that happened."

Freddie sat up and greedily eyed the proffered gifts.

"Anyway how come you're bringing cake?

You're not due in till five."

"Ann wanted me to remind you its six o'clock."

"Seriously?"

"She also said you've been away with the fairies and giggling all afternoon."

"I think I'm just tired matey, it's been a hectic week."

"A likely story."

Brian sat on the edge of the desk and gave him his best 'you can't fool me' look.

"Dreaming the day away with a daft faraway smile on your mush doesn't say tired to me, so I'm guessing its love. Care to share?"

"There's no new 'who' Bri so don't get any ideas, I'm still a one woman man."

"So what then?"

"I couldn't possibly say anything until after this delicious cake, and don't you dare tell Lisa."

Freddie scoffed the illicit treat while telling Brian all about his eventful day.

After many years as work colleagues they were also good friends and regularly confided their private lives to each other. Brian already knew about the baby thing so telling him about the visit to the doctor was no big deal.

But his phone faux par was a different matter, and eventually Brian had stopped laughing.

"I always knew Oscar liked you, but I didn't realise there was more to it than that."

"Even if there was, which there isn't, my dress sense is way too conservative for him, and I don't have tantrums...he can't exist without drama."

"Well that's good to hear."

"Why?"

"Well if you really want to know the truth I'd be exceptionally jealous if that devilishly handsome queen was after you, instead of me."

Brian shook his head, he looked genuinely disappointed.

"Really? All these years and I never realised you fancied..."

Freddie stopped short as someone in a hurry came barging into the green room.

"Ah there you are Freddie. I was hoping I'd find you here. Can I have a quick word?"

Alan Hopkin, chairman of the Swelford Amateur Musical Players who were currently staging Oklahoma in the theatre, was looking very flustered as he lumbered towards them.

At over six feet tall and about the same across, this giant of a man was normally a very gentle and calm individual, a complete contrast to his outward appearance which could terrorise anyone who didn't know him well.

Most of the time he always sported the broadest of smiles, but at this moment his face displayed a look of worry tinged with a slight expression of panic.

"Hi Alan."

Freddie greeted him with his best customer service persona.

"You're in early this evening, no more problems, I hope?"

"Not really, except that this show's been a complete fiasco Freddie. We seem to have staggered from one stupid crisis to another. It's probably the worst show I've ever been involved with."

"I'm hoping you not trying to blame us."

"Oh absolutely not Freddie, I didn't mean it like that. You and your guys have been terrific as always. But our own gremlins have been hard at work for quite some time now and we've had an extra share of bad luck this week, what with Banksy leaving us in the lurch and that ridiculous gun incident the other night."

"But it was very funny," Brian added hoping to lighten Alan's mood.

"It would have been if we were putting on a farce Brian, but Oklahoma was never meant to be a frivolous show."

"I totally agree Alan," Brian said.

"It's not an out and out comedy for sure, but it is supposed to be light-hearted and entertaining. The show I've been watching from out front has been neither."

"Sorry Alan," Freddie butted in.

"It's not really our place to comment Bri."

"No Freddie it's really okay, he's absolutely right."

"Sorry Alan, my mouth tends to work on its own without any input from my brain. But from what I've seen and heard it feels like the company have lost interest, both on and off stage."

"Trust me Brian we're all still interested but somehow we've lost our way so badly we can't see a way out. And since 'you know who' quit there's been an intense feeling of resentment throughout."

"But I don't understand," Freddie said.

"You've been telling me for years the committee were desperate to be rid of him. Surely he's done you all a big favour by walking out like that. So why all the fuss?"

"Probably because the damage is already done, and we've gone beyond the point when there's something worth salvaging."

"I don't agree. You still have some decent talent even if it is a little aged. You just need some fresh ideas, match the show to the people you've got, that's all."

"But we don't know how to Freddie. We're all over sixty, except Claire and she's no spring chicken. We're not the kind of group that could get away with doing any of the livelier modern scripts, so frankly I don't see how we're ever going to get our audiences back?"

"Unless you start doing something completely different," Freddie said thoughtfully.

He had a notion that there was an opportunity here that they were all overlooking somehow. But now wasn't the time as he was wondering if Alan's visit had a purpose or was he just getting things off his chest?

"It may all be a bit too late Freddie, and this will probably be our last production. The cast need to know the truth if we're going to go out on a positive note."

"When it comes to memories 'what a shame' is much better than 'thank god'."

"That's so true Freddie and very witty, can I use that saying?"

"It's far too clever to be one of his own so why not." Brian was looking at his watch.

"And on that note we need to press on guys, its quarter past already and the house opens in forty five, so don't keep him talking too long please Alan, there's still lots to do."

"We need to sort that gun out Freddie. Martha finds it really hard to use," Alan said as Brian left.

"For tonight I've got her a dummy pistol to use and added a gunshot sound effect to the show disc, that should make it easier and I'll let her know."

"She'll be relieved, thanks."

"So tell me Alan I'm curious to know why this could be your last production. Surely you just need to find a new director."

"There's no money left Freddie. Productions costs have gone through the roof and attendance is worse than ever. Every member has contributed an extra fifty pounds this year just to keep things going. If we manage a few more sales we might just break even, but it's not looking promising unless we can get some help."

Now Freddie knew why he wanted a quick word.

"So you need me to approach the trustees for a discount?"

"Would you?"

"How much are we talking about?"

"About five hundred."

That's not too bad Freddie thought, he knew for that amount he could probably help, but there would have to be conditions.

"Look," he said as quietly as possible just in case of radar ears.

"There'll be a better chance if you stop talking about this being your last show. It's good for business if the board drop prices to keep a good customer happy, but if this same client is insisting they won't return, then where's the incentive?"

"That makes sense."

"You're a really nice bunch of people Alan and

we've had some fun over the years, SAMPs is an institution and we'd all be sad to see you go. So get them all motivated and finish the job properly and I'll promise to get the finance sorted. Okay?"

"Thanks Freddie, really appreciated."

The chairman turned to go.

"And thank honest Brian for me as well."

7.00 pm – With all the pre-show checks complete and the stage set ready for the evening performance, Freddie was alone in the relative seclusion of the back office instead of at his usually station on stage, trying to enjoy a quiet coffee.

He was still considering the earlier conversation and the thought of losing another regular customer, the potential impact on the business was quite unsettling.

Brian's head appeared round the partition.

"Thirty minutes Freddie darling," he said.

"The foyers starting to fill up so we need to get the hoi polloi moving into the bar."

"Will do matey." Freddie was grateful to be distracted from his thoughts.

"Unless you think it would be much better to cancel the show, refund their money and send them home," Brian added sarcastically.

"Kinder too. I'm sure torturing paying customers is illegal, but that would hardly be a good decision for this cash guzzling venue, would it?"

"I really wouldn't worry about the audience Freddie. It's mainly been family and friends coming through the doors this week, and they're only here out of duty."

"Don't they deserve the one hundred percent

effort you were talking about earlier, for the support they've shown over the years?"

"I suppose, yes. But on the other hand, if they can't be honest enough to tell their nearest and dearest that they sing like the cat and have the acting ability of a door knob then they deserve to be punished and parted from their hard earned readies. After all someone has to pay our wages."

"And what of the future Bri?"

Freddie looked thoughtfully at his friend.

"Who'll pay our wages when all these small societies are gone If you think about it we actually need the likes of SAMPS if we're going to survive."

The potential of this scenario was nothing new to either of them, it was a regular topic of conversation. But it was always supposition, a concern rather than a definite outcome. Unfortunately, after today's events Freddie thought the possibility seemed closer to reality than ever before.

"I know you're right and it hadn't escaped my attention either. But what can we do?"

"Probably nothing, but it doesn't stop me thinking we should do something."

"Well if Alan's had a word then we can hope attitudes are somewhat better tonight, that would be a start."

"I doubt that'll be anywhere near enough somehow. You should have seen them during warm-up. As far as they're concerned not only has the fat lady sung but she also stolen all their polo mints and buggered off home."

"Is it really that bad?"

"I came back here just as Alan was having 'a word'. Why do you think I'm hiding?"

"I thought it was because you wanted to see more of wonderful old me."

As he'd said this Brian had flung his arms wide, but when Freddie didn't react his shoulders slumped and his smile disappeared.

"Another fifteen minutes Mr Grumpy and you can get the punters into their seats. Come on, just three more performances and you can pack the ill-fated Oldklahoma back into a lorry and wave it goodbye. You know better than to worry about things we have no control over."

Brian opened the bottom draw of his desk and pulled out a half bottle of Martell.

"And wash my mug out when you're finished and put a brandy in it ready for the interval."

"Well that's very kind of you but I really shouldn't drink during..."

"The brandy's for me you cheeky little shit. I have to watch this drivel every night in the stalls and trust me it's been agony. If anyone should get a refund it's me."

He banged the bottle down and headed back to the foyer to organise his volunteers.

"I know, I know."

Freddie laughed, lifted his head and started clapping.

"I've just been yanking your chain as usual," he called after his friend.

Freddie picked up the nearby microphone and reaching over to a switch panel he flicked the one marked 'Front of House' to the on position.

"Good evening ladies and gentlemen and welcome to The Hidden Theatre Company for this evening's exciting

performance of Oklahoma, brought to you by Swelford Amateur Musical Players. The house will open for you to take your seats in fifteen minutes. In the meantime why not consider avoiding the interval rush by pre-ordering your drinks at the bar. The curtain will rise for act one in thirty minutes, that's thirty minutes please, thank you."

Freddie turned 'Front of House' off and 'Back Stage' on. It was time to wake up the cast and rally the crew.

"This is your thirty minute call ladies and gentlemen, the house will open in fifteen minutes and so far ticket sales stand at thirty five percent for tonight's performance. All crew stations make your final checks please and clear the stage. Thirty minutes stand-by please, Thirty minutes thank you."

He would have normally made these announcements from his own control desk on the stage. But tonight an argument had broken out as the cast had been warming up on stage.

It concerned a particular scene and who was supposed to be standing where and the order in which they were meant to go on and when.

It would normally be for the director to sort out these issues, but of course they didn't have one so they turned to the stage manager.

"Freddie can you come and sort this out? Some of these fools are trying to make a meal out of their insignificant role, too much self indulgence if you ask me."

There had been some shouting and threats made after this remark, and it had turned quite nasty.

Freddie had reprimanded them.

"Everyone is important to the success of the show," he'd said. "And you've all been rehearsing for months, plenty of time to know what you're supposed to be doing and when. If you don't then I suggest you don't have a place on my stage."

Then Alan had appeared and roared his displeasure at their behaviour.

"Over here folks, gather round please, we need to have a serious talk."

Freddie had decided he needed a few moments of peace and didn't want to hang about to witness any commotion. So he'd put Steve in charge and headed for the back office.

"Call me on the radio if I'm needed but otherwise you can take a turn in dealing with all this pointless shit. After all it's partly your fault that Banksy quit."

He wasn't expecting to be called.

Nine

7.08 pm - The two-way radio hanging from his belt spat into life.

"Stage to SM."

Freddie picked up and pressed the talk button.

"Go ahead."

"Where are you Boss? We need some advice on the stage."

Freddie jumped to his feet.

The specific phrase 'we need some advice' was only used in an emergency and meant there was a serious problem on or close to the stage. Several of these radios were in use throughout the building and car park so Freddie knew not to ask any questions on the open channel, he would have to wait until he got there to find out how serious the crisis was.

"On my way," he confirmed and clipped the radio back on his belt.

As he left the office he grabbed the large first aid kit and defibrillator. Steve sounded worried and on the few occasions they'd used this coded message it had been the result of a medical incident.

By the time he arrived on the stage news had reached the dressing rooms that something terrible had happened and most of the cast were gathering to gawp.

"Why is it that folk like to stare at the misfortunes of others?" Freddie said as he nudged his way past the worried onlookers. Even though he still didn't know what had actually happened, he was guessing that with all the yelling and swearing someone must be in pain. That much was obvious.

"Be a bit more careful you clumsy bugger, that really hurts." Bob the lead of the show was the one expressing his displeasure.

"Well at least he's breathing," Freddie said as he put the kit bags down next to Steve. "Yelling is always a good sign."

Bob was lying on the floor almost up against his scooter. Steve had already managed to expose the injury by cutting off Bob's light stage shoe and sock, and was now gently holding two ice-packs around the noticeably ballooning ankle which he'd supported and elevated by wrapping a couple of blankets around and under the injured limb.

"Get this moron away from me."

"Why?" Freddie asked sharply. "Looks to me like he's doing a good job there."

"Well he doesn't have the first idea about what he's doing. He should never have taken my shoe off. I can't tell you how much pain it caused me."

"Then don't tell me because I'm not really interested. See how swollen your foot is Bob? Well by now your toes would be going numb if he hadn't removed it."

Steve looked up at the boss and mouthed the words 'thank you'.

"So what are you thinking?" Freddie asked.

"Well I think he owes me for a new pair of..."

"Not you Bob, I was asking Steve. How bad is it?" Bob scowled at them both.

"Not sure boss, it's quite swollen as you can see. I was just here when it happened. As he stood up his foot wasn't fully on the scooter platform and his leg just seemed to twist and slip off. He gave quite a yelp when it hit the floor."

"No choice then, I'll phone for an ambulance."

Freddie turned to the cast. "Whichever one of you is Bob's understudy you'll need to get ready to take over for tonight's show."

"There isn't one."

Alan the chairman was pushing his way to the front of the group, stopping to stare in horror at his injured leading man.

"What, you've got no understudy for the lead?"

"We did have, but the old git got taken into a care home two weeks ago and obviously no one thought about a replacement. How bad is it Bob?"

"Now chummy boy here has stopped wagging it about, it's not so bad."

"Well maybe you should be nice to 'chummy boy' as it would have hurt a lot more if I'd had to take that shoe off now," Alan said as he manoeuvred his large bulky frame down and onto the floor beside the prone casualty.

Steve's smile was massive. Now two people had clearly stated that he'd done the right thing.

But Freddie was a little confused as to why Alan was getting involved. He turned to his grinning fly captain. "I think you'd better go and call the ambulance," he said.

"Wait just a minute please."

Alan's tone was quite brusque and brought Steve to an abrupt halt before he'd even had chance to stand up. He definitely wasn't going to argue with the big man.

"Come on Alan we haven't got a clue how bad that ankle is," Freddie chipped in. "He needs to be seen by a medical professional."

"And a doctor's going to take a look at it now Freddie, if everyone will shut up for a minute and let me."

"Blimey, don't tell me you're a doctor as well?"

"As well as what?" Alan mused.

"Oh never mind," Freddie turned to Steve, "Every time you turn around up pops another doctor you knew nothing about."

"Consultant actually," Alan said cheerily then lowered his voice to a stage whisper, "But we prefer to stay incognito otherwise we spend all day bombarded by Mrs Friend's varicose veins and Mr Acquaintance's haemorrhoids."

He gave Steve a knowing wink.

Steve looked confused, he was wondering how Alan knew about his haemorrhoids.

"Did you hear or feel it snap Bob?" Alan asked.

"It all happened so quickly, but no I don't think so. It's just throbbing at the moment, but it's definitely getting more painful."

"Let's have a good look at it then."

Putting the ice packs to one side Alan started to feel all around the ankle as Bob reconvened his barrage of abuse at the intrusive prodding. After a minute or so the examination was over and Alan looked up and loudly announced,

"Well you'll all be pleased to know I don't think it's broken, I'm sure it's just a bad sprain. So we don't need an ambulance after all Freddie. A couple of wide elasticated bandages and some tape from your kit will do the trick and he'll be as good as new and ready to perform in no time at all."

"Ready to do what?" Bob exclaimed, but was ignored.

"And you'll fill in the accident book to that effect Alan," Freddie said, knowing he needed to ensure no liability could be attached to the theatre or staff.

"Just get Steve to fill it out now and I'll happily sign it."

"Surely you're not expecting me to go on stage like this Alan," Bob spoke up. "I doubt I can walk on it, it's very painful you know."

"Well you'll have to grin and bear it Bob, the show must go on and all that. Lets' get you strapped up and see how well you can walk."

Steve had removed the packaging from two large crepe bandages and passed them over to Alan who now started to carefully wrap one around Bob's damaged limb.

Freddie had an idea. "Don't you think it would be a better if..."

His words were cut short as Alan grabbed his elbow and leant in close.

"Help us out here Freddie, please remember what I said earlier. We must do the show if it's at all possible. Let me strap him up and then we'll see if he can walk, and if not then..."

"Well," said Freddie, a bit miffed about being

interrupted, especially as he was about to reveal an idea which might help the situation.

"I was just trying to say, don't you think it would be better if he used his scooter?"

"To do what?" Alan paused his methodical strapping.

"To get him out on that stage to play Curly of course. Even if he can put weight on his ankle he's not going to last two and a half hours on it, is he?"

"Probably not, no. But I thought you had to do a risk assessment to use any motorised equipment on the stage."

"You do, but we had a company last year that put on a play using scooters, so the assessment has already been done. So it's an option."

Bob tossed his eyes and tutted.

"It would look out of place and stupid in a show like this," he said cynically. "You must be joking."

"No, no I'm not Bob. Over the years I've seen so many weird things on this stage that it's made me realise it doesn't matter what you do as long as it's entertaining. Standing or sitting, you can still perform."

Bob still looked unconvinced.

"Look chap," Freddie continued. "This really is none of my business and I should just walk away and leave you all to make your own decisions. But make them quickly as the paying public out front are expecting a show in less than twenty minutes. I'm just trying to be practical and help you find a workable solution."

"I think we could really use Banksy's advice right now, he'd know what to do."

"That's rubbish Bob and you know it," Alan

snapped. "Anyway he's not here so the decision has to be ours."

"So what are the choices other than to use the scooter or cancel."

The gathered cast, who'd been listening quietly to this exchange of words, now started to join in. They obviously wanted a say about any decision that was going to be made.

"You're out and about on that scooter all the time Bob," Elsa one of the elderly dancers said.

"The audience will understand the need for you to use it," said another.

"But a modern scooter hardly fits in with hay bales and horse drawn surreys does it?" Bob insisted. "I just think it needs to be relevant and believable."

"Oh do you mean believable as in pensioners gingerly inching themselves around the stage trying to act like love struck, hormone soaked teenagers?" Alan said, as he finished strapping Bob's ankle.

He rose to his feet. "Theatre is fantasy and not reality Bob. Freddie's right, the punters just want to be entertained."

Freddie suddenly had another idea.

"Tell you what," he announced looking pleased with himself.

"We've got two or three Zimmer frames and some old walking sticks in the property store. What do you think about Bob going out on his scooter and the rest of you using the props to play Oklahoma as yourselves. Give the audience OLDkahoma. Perform it as you've all been joking about it."

"Now you're just being stupid."

"No Bob, stupid would be suggesting we disguise your scooter by dressing it in the pantomime horse costume. Like I said I really am trying to be helpful here."

"And we're grateful," Alan quickly interjected. "But the fact remains that we haven't got time to change anything or alter the script."

"I'm not suggesting that Alan, just hear me out for a minute. Oklahoma is all about young love and jealousy, the angst and pride of young folk trying to find their position in life. Now, think about how you've struggled to get much of a response from the spectators so far this week and ask the question 'what can we do to make the best of what we've got?' And that's the paradox Alan, I'm suggesting you use the irony of this situation and play the original script, but as yourselves, an older wiser generation reliving the exuberance of youth, or at least trying to."

"It wouldn't work, the audience will just laugh us off the stage," said Bob.

"I think that's part of the plan," Claire joked. "It would be very funny though."

The rest of the cast all started excitedly talking at once.

"Yes, that's a great idea...Play to that...It'll get a laugh for sure...Let's do it...Better than cancelling."

"But how do we do this Freddie?" Claire shouted above the din.

It suddenly went quiet, all eyes on their new inspiration.

"Surely love and jealousy applies to everyone and not just the young. So look and behave like the older generation you are. In this business we're so busy trying to get into character that we don't notice what's going on around us. So just be what and who you are instead of what you think you should be.

Speak the lines and sing the songs exactly as it is in the script, but the difference will be what the audience sees. Be old and fragile, forget the wigs and let the make-up say old. Wear glasses and if you have a stick or frame use it. If walking and dancing makes you tired then exaggerate it. If you perform it like you mean it then your audience will believe it."

The whole group was transfixed and no one spoke for what seemed ages.

Alan broke the silence. "I think it's brilliant Freddie. Come on guys and gals I really think we should do this, I certainly want to, and if nothing else let's get out there and have some fun. Freddie, Steve let's get Bob back on his bus."

"Don't I get a say in any of this?"

"Of course Bob," Alan replied. "Because you're the one having to bear the burden of leading this project, you should get the biggest say."

Alan paused, caught Freddie's eye and continued, "But I'm sure you're more than a good enough actor to pull this off."

"You're right," Bob beamed proudly. "Come on quickly help me up."

When Bob was back on his scooter and everyone was busy recreating themselves, Freddie had called Geoff the Musical Director to the stage to explain what was going on. Even though it didn't affect the score, Freddie thought it best to let him know beforehand that the cast hadn't gone completely mad.

Geoff was an ex-pro from the West End, but nowadays there were few openings for those fast approaching fifty, which he was, unless you were famous, which he wasn't.

Now he makes a living as a professional Musical Director.

In times long past Freddie and Geoff had worked together on stage. Geoff had looked out for this younger performer, showing him the ropes and getting him into trouble on many occasions. All these years later and their friendship has lasted, and still gets them into trouble, mainly at the many after show parties at THTC.

Freddie had just finished telling him what was happening when Alan the chairman joined them, once again in a hurry, with another request.

"We're going to need a few more minutes Freddie. Bob wants to have a quick practice manoeuvring around the set and the cast have gone back to the dressing rooms to change their makeup and stuff."

"Steve's just given the fifteen Alan and most of the audience have taken their seats already."

"No worries," Geoff said in his rich Irish accent. "I'll buy you five minutes, if that's okay?"

"That should be plenty."

"Call a short tech delay exactly on time Freddie, and I'll tell you what I've got planned. But first I'm going to need a walking stick, a handful of snow powder. Then I've got to get down to make-up pronto."

"You've always liked a bit of blusher matey."

"Aye Freddie, I do...Reminds me of the good times."

Ten

7.30 pm - As arranged, Freddie made the announcement.

"Ladies and Gentlemen if I could have your attention for a moment please. Due to a small technical problem there will be a short delay to the start of tonight's performance. Thank you."

Backstage Freddie could hear the murmurs of discontent coming from the audience and he smiled to himself as he moved the microphone away from his mouth and partially covered it with his hand, but he deliberately left the switch in the on position. He spoke frantically, but to no one in particular.

"Well where is he? He can't have gone far for goodness sake, get out there and find him."

Out in the auditorium the attending could still hear the announcer's voice coming over the public address system, it sounded like some kind of muffled panic.

More weird sounds were coming out of the speakers, but this was just Freddie deliberately tapping the live microphone on his knee and rubbing it on his clothes.

Then another voice from somewhere in the background shouted,

"Boss, boss they can hear you out front, turn the microphone off."

There was a pause, some inaudible muttering and a final loud click.

Everyone back stage heard the ripple of laughter coming through the show relay monitors as it coursed around the auditorium. Freddie turned to look at those standing ready in the wings, heads together enjoying the moment, he could sense a renewed excitement, anticipation in the face of the upcoming challenge, and suddenly there it was.

He could feel the buzz.

This, he thought, was why he loved his job.

At that very moment Geoff the MD had stumbled into the auditorium through a side door in clear view of everyone waiting for the show to begin.

What they saw appeared to be a grey haired old man dressed in a black tuxedo and bow tie. He had a seriously extreme case of dandruff and was almost bent double over a walking stick as he shuffled a few paces forward till he reached row D.

Everyone stopped chattering and laughing to stare in wonder at this unexpected spectacle.

"I appear to be a bit lost," he croaked at the couple sitting in the end seats.

"I don't suppose you know where I need to go."

Scotty, unmistakable dressed as a member of the crew in the typical black garb and carrying a two-way radio, came hurrying through the same door and grabbed Geoff by the arm.

He spoke into the radio.

"I've found him Boss."

"Then get him in the pit."

Came the reply over the device, the volume turned up full for maximum effect.

"Come on Geoff, let's get you in place."

Scotty started to lead the seemingly aged gent slowly toward the front of the stage.

There was another ripple of laughter, this time accompanied by sporadic applause.

"You're a very nice young man sonny, thank you," Geoff kept repeating as they passed down the aisle. He stopped at the end of another row of seats to shower the occupants with dandruff and pose them the question,

"Don't you think he's a very nice young man?"

They nodded in agreement through the cloud of white flakes and Geoff moved on still chattering away merrily.

At THTC the orchestra pit in front of the stage comprises of a platform on a hydraulic lift, allowing it to be positioned at any level depending on whether the director wants the musicians to be seen or not.

For this show, Geoff had set it a couple of feet below the level of the main auditorium floor, and a curtained rail was in place to screen everything but his head and shoulders.

As the pair approached the side steps down into the pit, the walking stick seemed to suddenly slip sideways and the old man lost his balance. Despite Scotty's desperate attempt to grab him, Geoff fell through the curtain and into the pit with a yell of terror.

The audience gasped as one and several of them

stood, craning their necks to see where he'd gone.

Geoff kept them waiting just a few seconds then jumped to his feet and waved his arms amid another huge shower of dandruff, his head just popping over the top of the curtain rail.

"I'm okay, I'm okay. Nothing broken, I don't think," he called out.

Again there was laughter and applause from the assembled crowd.

Freddie and Alan were watching all of this on the monitors at the control desk, and many of the cast were doing the same around the backstage area.

"I told you he was a genius," Freddie said to the chairman as they watched Geoff climb cautiously into position on his rostrum, helped by Scotty and the prompt lady.

"He's not the only one."

Alan thumped Freddie's back.

"Thanks Boss. This might work out okay after all."

"I'm sure it will Alan."

He adjusted his headset and through it spoke to his crew,

"Have a good one everybody, standby we're set. Starting positions please and house lights travelling."

He reached over and started pressing buttons.

As the house lights dimmed, the audience settled ready for the show to begin.

Geoff raised his baton preparing the orchestra to begin the overture.

"So how's your old man then?"

An elderly sounding female voice rang out clearly from the pit.

"Oh he's not too bad," was the creaky reply.

"But he's having a bit of trouble with his waterworks. Still, mustn't grumble eh."

"Shush," Geoff said loudly and tapped his baton on his music stand.

That was Freddie's cue. He turned the 'Auditorium' switch back to the on position.

"Ladies and Gentlemen if I could have your attention for one moment please. We would like to apologise for the short delay to the start of tonight's performance, this was owing to a small technical problem. Having now resolved that matter Swelford Amateur Musical Players are proud to present, 'Oldklahoma'."

Geoff swung his baton with exaggerated gusto and the twelve piece band launched into the overture as the audience looked quizzically at each other.

Had they heard that right?

Oldklahoma?

Four and a bit minutes later the overture finished and as the audience showed their appreciation Geoff turned to face them to take a bow.

To everyone's amusement he was wearing an oxygen mask and looked exhausted.

The volume of the applause increased dramatically.

The music began again, but this time all quiet and atmospheric as the pit lights dimmed and the stage tabs opened.

The stage lit up to reveal a somewhat dishevelled farmhouse with what looked to be a very old lady draped over a butter churn, a Zimmer frame close at hand.

She appeared to be sleeping but suddenly stirred from her stupor and frantically started cranking the handle on the butter churn as the music stopped.

Hidden from view behind the house Curly started singing the opening lines of 'Oh what a beautiful morning'.

"There's a...."

As he sang each line of the first verse the butter churning slowed and by the end the old lady was asleep again.

When it was time for the main chorus Curly, aka Bob, made his entrance from behind the house.

"Oh what...."

He sang lustily as he punched the drive button and lurched forward on the scooter,

"Oh what...."

But he'd misjudged his speed, overshot the gap he was supposed to use as his entrance and ploughed straight through the small picket fence next to the house reducing it to match wood.

But he kept going.

"I've got...."

Aunt Eller, the butter churn lady, quickly moved her feet out of the way just in time to prevent them from being crushed, and as Bob sped across the stage she shook her fist at him.

As he finished the chorus Bob took his finger off the button and came to an abrupt halt just short of the raised lip at the front of the stage.

He faced his enthralled public.

"All the...."

Most of the audience were now in stitches as Curly the cowboy continued his song.

Freddie was watching his monitor intently, certain that Bob's expression might actually mean he was enjoying himself.

"All the...."

Bob spread his arms and smile wide and gave it everything.

"They don't...."

But Freddie could see the actor had made a serious error in the positioning of his scooter. Bob too had realised this and a look of horror was spreading across his face.

But still he continued.

"Oh what...."

There wasn't enough room to drive forward.

"Oh what...."

The only way he could move was backward.

"I've got...."

So Bob was going to have to reverse the scooter.

It would soon be very obvious that everything wasn't going his way.

As the music continued Bob reached down and turned the switch on the handle of his scooter from forward to reverse.

He had no choice.

Both he and Freddie knew from experience what was about to happen.

This next verse was supposed to be sung all softly and sweetly.

"All the...."

Bob yelled tunelessly instead. He had to cover his mistake.

"All the...."

He stabbed his finger on the drive lever, the scooter lurched backward.

'Beep, beep, beep'

The scooter joined in, also out of tune.

"The...."

'This vehicle is reversing'

The scooter had its own version of the song.

"And a...."

'Beep, beep, beep'

But nothing could be heard of either as the audience were in hysterics.

"Oh what...."

As Bob took his finger off the button he'd stopped right next to Aunt Eller who was trying to hide in her apron,

"I've got...."

A resigned Bob put the smile back on Curly's face and finished the song.

As the opening number concluded the audience erupted into applause. Brian was standing at the back of the auditorium, mopping at the tears streaming down his face.

And so the show continued, no one fooled around or over-acted but rather noticeably emphasised the script, just as Freddie had suggested. Every member of the cast played their part in a production that had suddenly come alive.

Martha, the sprightly seventy four year old grandmother, playing the part of Aunt Eller added a little of her natural dry humour to the proceedings, occasionally warbling, "I'm nearly eighty seven don't you know," at the end of her lines.

It was made even funnier as each time she did this the number had increased and by the end of the third scene she'd reached the "Grand ole age of ninety three."

The audience loved it and sang along with the songs and even winced a little out of embarrassment as the elderly Curly and Laurey openly displayed feelings of desire and passion towards each other. They played it so well that somehow it felt completely wrong, and yet so sweet. In fact the audience became so involved that they even started to jeer and hiss panto style at Jud the farm hand, who by simply adding a crumpled raincoat and flat cap to his wardrobe had managed to transform his bland obsessive stalker of a character, into a despised creepy old letch.

The whole performance provoked a variety of emotions, as any good musical should, but mainly the audience laughed.

When Ali Hakim the Persian peddler substituted the scripted present of a garter to Aunt Eller for a pair of surgical stockings they'd chuckled, and when he'd attempted to put them on her, they'd howled.

Even funnier was after he'd sold the magic potion to Laurey that was supposed to reveal her true love, he'd held up another glass vial and stated, "And when you've captured your man, here's a mystical blend from the east, formulated to kindle the fire in his loins."

"What's it called?" she'd asked.

"They call it Viagreeee," was the reply.

"My oh my," hollered Aunt Eller.

"I could sure find use for some of that."

"Couldn't we all love," a familiar voice from the pit shouted.

At the interval Brian had come backstage.

"What's going on? Who's kidnapped the cast of SAMPs and saved the day? The excitement in the bar is unbelievable."

"They're doing okay I reckon."

"Okay? They're doing better than okay, and the best of it is there are two reporters in tonight. They want pictures, so I've just introduced them to Alan."

"Good, let's hope they get a good write-up, they certainly deserve one."

The second half was just as good with the audience continuing to show their appreciation. Everything seemed a little bit chaotic, but it was delivered well, the cast stayed in character and that had made it all work perfectly.

But the stars of the show were undoubtedly Curly and his trusty steed. Bob was concentrating so hard on his performance that his driving was nothing short of dreadful. Folk constantly had to jump out of the way to avoid being flattened and he even managed to take great chunks out of the scenery. But this seemed to endow the scooter with its very own personality and it often set off in a direction or at a speed Curly was obviously not expecting.

Then just as he came off stage to get ready for the finale the battery died, but it didn't matter.

Freddie quickly organised four members of the cast to just push Bob and his scooter on stage, and they'd fitted it with a 'fringe on top'.

The small audience stood as one to applaud at the walk down, saving the biggest cheer for Curly and the scooter.

Alan was the first off the stage to acknowledge the real hero of the hour.

"Bravo Freddie, brilliant idea. But look at Bob's face. He was a diva before, now you've unleashed a monster, for which I am truly thankful."

Eleven

Saturday 30th 8.55 am - Freddie was standing alone in an irregularly shaped room which appeared mainly drab and undecorated.

In each of the many nondescript walls were several plain white doors, some furnished with well worn and tarnished brass handles, some unembellished and featureless.

In the centre of the room a wide open plan staircase with white metal handrails and unpolished wooden treads ascended in a sweeping arc into a dark upper level.

The whole area was empty except for an occasional small puddle of decrepit and unusable old furniture, along with several empty picture frames hanging at precarious angles on one of the far walls.

In total contrast to the lacklustre décor, the floor of the room was covered with brightly coloured carpets and many patterned rugs. Although there was nothing to define this room as anywhere in particular or anything special, every aspect of it was most definitely of great significant to its owner.

This was Freddie's private room, conceived in his own imagination, in his latest dream.

Freddie had always been a vivid dreamer.

Why was he here and why did it feel like he was desperately searching for something...but what?

He wandered aimlessly around for what seemed like ages, trying to decide which door to open in an attempt to discover an answer to this question, then finally found himself at the bottom of the staircase, looking up into a dark, foreboding abyss.

......*'Maybe it's time to be brave' a voice said. 'you might find a conclusion to this search in the lofty heights of this secret hideaway'*......

In a moment of abandon he grabbed the cold metal handrail, but as he placed his right foot on the first tread he became rooted to the spot as a sudden feeling of absolute dread coursed across his shoulders and down his back.

"What shall I do?" he heard himself say in a very tremulous voice.

"Well you could sit up and take this off me," came the unexpected reply.

He knew the voice but as he looked around his lovely wife was nowhere to be seen, and now he heard her warmly chuckling.

"Come on sleepy head, open your eyes. Get back here and help me out."

He opened the eyes he already thought were open, and uncertainty suddenly became reality.

He was in his bed all cosy and warm, the ever present sweet smell of vanilla reminding him he was definitely at home.

"Good morning my tousled knight in shining,"

the lovely Lisa announced in her light sing-song voice as she stood looking down at him. She was holding a tray.

Freddie wearily repositioned his pillows and sat up in bed so she could place the tray down on his outstretched legs. He noted the presence of two bowls full of intriguing looking goodies and steaming mugs of something dark and fragrant, all of which he'd never seen the like of before.

Maybe this was still a dream after all.

"I thought it might be nice to have breakfast in bed this morning," she said sweetly. "And it'll give us a chance to discuss our new plan," she added with a smile as she transferred the drinks from the tray to the bedside table.

"Ah, so you have a new plan you want to tell me about then."

Picking up a teaspoon he started to explore the unusual contents of one of the bowls by prodding at it.

"And discuss?" he joked. "That's a word I haven't heard in a very long while."

"Your unique brand of sarcasm is as cutting as ever Mr Hobbs," Lisa teased, trying hard to sound offended but failing badly.

"You make me sound such a right bossy madam."

"You bossy? Never."

"What never?"

"Well…hardly ever."

Lisa moved round to her side of the bed, made herself comfortable and then took the other bowl and spoon from off the tray.

"So come on, what's the new plan then?"

"How we're going to get me pregnant," she replied light heartedly. "Unless you can come up with a better plan for a lazy Saturday morning in bed?"

Freddie suddenly lost all interest in his bowl of weirdness.

"What could be better than a bit of morning frolicking with my sexy lady, and it's definitely something we have to do to get you pregnant. I really like the new plan already. Get your jimjams off then."

"There's a bit more to it than that Mr Impatient. There's already been plenty of frolicking without any success, so we need to add a few more details. The plan needs expanding a bit, or maybe even a lot."

"I'm expanding as we speak, how big a plan will you need?"

"You'll have to wait a bit Freddie." She was giggling but her voice was resolute. "And you'll need to stop waving it around randomly. We need to set an effective routine and then stick to it."

"You make it all sound like it needs to be a well executed military operation as opposed to something that should just happen naturally."

"But it hasn't happened naturally Freddie, nothing's happening."

Her mood had suddenly changed, the jovial chirpiness of before was replaced with obvious irritation.

Freddie dropped his head and started pushing the contents of his bowl around again.

"Sorry," he said sheepishly.

She took a deep breath and composed herself. An argument was the last thing she wanted and it certainly wouldn't help the situation anyway.

"Me too," she gave him a soft smile and her eyes crinkled at the corners.

"I really want a baby Freddie and you've said it's what you want too, AND, you also said you'll do whatever it takes to keep me happy, yes?"

"Always."

"I think we've both been a bit too lazy," the lovely Lisa continued. "Just expecting nature to take its course has been a useless misconception."

Freddie burst out laughing, "Missed conception, ha ha ha, I get it, so funny."

She didn't see the joke and scowled at his interruption.

"Sorry...again," he added quickly once he realised.

"I just think this month should signal a fresh start." She spoke positively, "We're going to be more focused and nothing will be overlooked or underdone in the quest for success. It's all about the planning. Routine and consistency will deliver the right outcome for sure. Are you with me on this?"

Freddie felt he would probably be beaten to death if he didn't fall in line and just about managed to resist the urge to salute.

"So I'm guessing this tray of mysterious artefacts is the start of the new plan," he said instead.

"What is it?"

"It's a mixture of oats, pumpkin and sunflower seeds, goja and acai berries, fresh figs, cranberries, hazelnuts and natural yogurt."

"And the drink?"

"Acacia and camomile flower infusion."

"And what's it all supposed to do?"

"It's not supposed to do anything specifically. I just thought it would be a healthy way to start today. Stop messing with it and eat it, you might even enjoy it."

"I doubt that very much." He lifted a spoonful to his nose and sniffed at it suspiciously.

"Just eat, it won't kill you," she poked him playfully with her spoon.

He quickly put the spoon in his mouth, sucked the contents off and chewed.

"Bloody hell that's sour," he spluttered.

"It's high in energy, antioxidants and vitamins. It'll give you some oomph."

"I didn't realise I needed any."

"And it might keep you away from that wretched toaster."

"More likely it'll make me want to sit in a bath full of water along with the toaster, still plugged in and switched on. This is horrible."

"But it's good for you."

"Why is it that everything that's good for me is either painful or disgusting?"

"Ah diddums and welcome to my world," she mocked.

"You're always saying how much you appreciate my gorgeously sexy body, well guess how I keep it that way? Certainly not with the same doorstep cheese sandwiches or burgers you're always stuffing in your face."

"Look, I've already said I'll try to be healthier but you know what my jobs like."

It was Freddie's turn to be defensive. "I eat 'on the go' so food I can carry around in one hand is required. Plus I don't have your resolve, I admit I'm weak and definitely couldn't eat this rubbish all the time."

"Do you men get these excuses from a handbook or something?" she mocked. "But okay, I realise that at work you do what you do. But to compensate I want you to eat food like this when you're at home. I know that your diet is probably the least of our problems but I'll be happy if you promise to try."

"You know I'll agree but please can it be a bit more palatable?"

She shrugged.

He took yet another mouthful to please her. "So what else does this plan involve?"

"Tell me you're enjoying it first."

"I'm enjoying it."

He was wincing at the sourness of the berries.

"Mmmmmm lovely."

"You used to be a great actor my sweet and loveable hubbie, but to be honest nowadays you're rubbish."

"I'm going to store this memory away in case I ever need to play a character being tortured to death by his uncaring heartless wife. Just tell me the rest of the plan before my tongue packs its bags and emigrates."

"Well for a start you ungrateful ham..."

"Hey, who you calling a ham? I was once considered a star. You just said so."

"OKAY, well for a start then you totally misguided loser…"

"Much better, thank you."

"You're welcome. For a start we're still going to have sex every day with you on top like before. I'm know Dr Yates told you every other day was enough, but I can't help feeling that the more often I get fresh healthy sperm from you the better chance they'll have of being in the right place at just the right moment."

"I'm not complaining, but I do hate being on top all the time."

"It's the best position, and we have to have sex only in the morning from now on Freddie, because that's when your sperm count supposed to be at its peak."

"Ah, that's not so good."

Freddie had deliberately not relayed that bit of his conversation with the doctor, and was wondering how Lisa had discovered that unwelcomed titbit of information.

"How early are we talking here?" he asked.

"Six, maybe earlier depending on my schedule."

"Why that early? It doesn't usually take me too long."

"Because I've got to stay lying on my back for a full half an hour afterwards, stops everything swimming the wrong way, if you get my drift?"

"At six in the morning I'm sure my guys will be a whole lot keener to drift than swim."

"FREDDIE," Lisa scolded, but couldn't hide her smile.

Freddie regularly worked until after midnight and would finally make it into his bed to sleep an hour or two later.

"I'm sorry about the timing sweetie, but it could make all the difference."

"How much difference is that really going to make, surely my sperm count just keeps increasing until we deliberately evict some of them?"

"I don't understand the science either Freddie, but I want us to follow the doctor's advice."

"Hang on, when did a doctor tell you that then? You said you weren't going until after I'd been fully checked out."

"I had lunch with Danni Yates yesterday."

"Lunch with our doctor? You never told me you knew her socially."

"I didn't until a couple of weeks ago, but there's been a growing interest around women's health issues over the last few years and we've lagged behind a bit, well a lot to be honest. I'd originally approached Danni as our local GP with a proposition to write a regular column for IGL. Hazel's great with relationship issues and stuff but when it comes to medical advice we really need to get a bone-fide professional opinion to avoid any potential litigation. I've met up with her a couple of times now and was really surprised to learn you two know each other quite well, or so she said."

"Yes I do know her very well, she's really nice."

"She speaks highly of you too, is there anything you haven't told me?"

"Don't be daft." Freddie hoped she wasn't referring to the 'morning sperm count' information and that his former backstage volunteer hadn't dropped him in it.

"Anyway I have told you about her," he added. "Remember Danni Moore? Well that's who she used to be, and trust me, no one was more surprised than when I walked through the surgery door and realised I was about to discuss my sex life with someone I knew well. So what else has she been telling you about me?"

"Nothing I haven't heard before really, at least no incriminating juicy gossip I can use against you."

"Well that's a relief because she knows most of the shocking truth."

Lisa ignored him, "So you're going to be okay with sex every morning."

"Was that a question or a statement? I couldn't really tell."

"Take it as you want, but you will be, won't you?"

"I suppose," he replied reluctantly,."I can live with the interruption to my slumbers if it's only for a while."

"At least you can go back to sleep after, I've got to stick a pillow under my bum and lie on my back for ages, I'm just hoping half an hour will be enough time even for your obviously exhausted and directionally challenged sperm to find and reach their target."

"Why don't we get them some miniature torches and maps just in case?"

"FREDDIE!"

"What about the pot then, when are we going to fill that?"

"Haven't you done that yet?"

"I was hoping…erm no sorry."

He unwittingly shovelled another spoonful from his bowl by way of an apology.

"Oh Freddie I thought we'd agreed that's something you need to do on your own. I'm certainly not prepared to assist any of the lazy little buggers to get a relaxing holiday in a clean and well lit plastic hotel. I know it has to be done but do it yourself, please, and soon."

There was an uncomfortable silence while they both took a drink and ate some more of Lisa's concoction. He hated seeing her disappointed especially when it was with him."

"So is that it then?" he muttered as he chewed. "Once a day in the morning and eat healthy, that's the new plan?"

Lisa sipped her drink and looked apologetic. There was definitely something else, he could sense it.

"I want you to keep an open mind on this one Freddie."

"Go on, I'm intrigued, honestly I am."

"I've been reading an article written by an eminent psychologist about the power of the mind. He suggests that we're able to control everything to do with our body purely by being confident and projecting positive thoughts."

"Oh you mean like a placebo effect? If you really believe something will work, it will."

"In a way yes. So I want you to believe you're going to produce good healthy sperm hell bent on their role to fertilise."

"Proven fact or just another piece of rag mag mumbo jumbo?"

"Does it matter if it works?"

Freddie didn't want to spoil Lisa's buoyant mood and delay the fun he was sure they we're about to have.

"Okay you're right, so when does this whole new routine start then?"

"Well they say there's no time like the present and you've been trying it on since you woke up."

"I think I've lost interest."

"Since when you liar, come here."

A few minutes later Freddie was feeling great. Being intimate with his beautiful wife would always feel special to him, even in this awkward position.

"Why does that cushion have to be there now, I thought you said you put it under your bum afterwards."

"It helps to tilt everything downhill and gravity helps your little lads to swim in the right direction."

"Oh, okay."

"Freddie?"

"What?" came the muffled reply.

He was trying to support his weight by using his head buried deep in the pillow.

"Remember what I said about being able to control everything to do with your body purely by being confident and projecting positive thoughts. You need to visualise healthy strong sperm leaving you and travelling through my womb, finding my egg and fertilising it."

"Seriously?"

"I'm not asking for the world sweetie, just try it for me, please."

"Oh okay."

"Thanks."

"Would it help if I think out loud?"

"Possibly, I suppose it doesn't hurt to try."

"Great, then I'm visualising the newest, strongest and fittest little swimmers making their way to the front of the group."

"That's good, project positivity to them."

"Hang on, there's one among them who is more determined than the rest, he's a champion, a winner, he wants to know if you're projecting positivity to your egg, is it ready for him."

"He's the one Freddie, my egg is ready."

"Then SuperSperm is masking up as we speak...he's on his way."

"Oh Freddie, grow up!"

Twelve

4.45 pm - Freddie picked up his coat and sandwich box, headed out of the kitchen and stopped in the hallway for another warm cuddle from his lovely wife.

For lunch Lisa had spoilt him by cooking his favourite roast beef dinner with huge fluffy Yorkshire puddings and thick rich gravy, followed by treacle sponge and custard.

They'd spent the afternoon cuddling on the sofa, watching old movies on the telly and chatting about Freddie's upcoming thirty seventh birthday, with Lisa keen to know what he wanted to do to celebrate.

"Something simple will suit me fine," he'd said. "Nothing elaborate and definitely no surprises," he'd insisted.

Now it was time for Freddie to head off to work.

"I've had a really nice day, especially that lunch, thank you."

"After all that we've done today Freddie Hobbs, and the only thing you mention is the food. You're so exasperating." She playfully smacked his bum then pushed him towards the front door.

"Apparently it's the only way to a man's heart, or so they say," he protested.

"It's not the only way though, is it?" She giggled as he fended off her attempted grab for his crotch.

"Hey hey stop it, you'll send me to work all pent up and frustrated if you mess around down there."

"Then you'll have to walk the streets of Swelford and find someone willing to relieve the situation, or maybe you could just ask Brian to help you out. Tell you what, take the sample pot with you."

"The gay men in my life don't need any encouragement from you my dear lady."

"From what I hear neither do you," she teased.

She helped him on with his coat.

"Any plans for tonight?" he asked.

That was a silly question really, she nearly always headed for her office in town or attended an important meeting when he went off to work.

"I'm meeting Oscar for cocktails at Chaplin's later. He wants me to take a look at a new designer for a feature."

Freddie immediately saw a glint in her eye and a slight blush on her cheeks.

"Go on," he said, "What's the rest?"

The colour of her blush darkened considerably.

The only time Lisa reacted like this was when she was hiding something, and it certainly wasn't Oscar, as lovely as she was she'd never be his type.

"It's nothing," she insisted. "Or at least it's nothing important."

"I'll see your secret and raise you a tickle then."

He made a grab for her but she turned and

wriggled away, forcing him to chase her through the open living room door and around the back of the sofa where he cornered her. It was playtime.

"Freddie, no, please, we don't have time for this."

She squealed like a little girl, then shrieked with laughter as he pinned her down. Wrapping his arms around her he started his tactile interrogation.

"No secrets between us, remember?" he said.

"It's a surprise Freddie, you love surprises."

She gave another squeak as he found a spot somewhere between 'ouch and ooh'.

"I hate surprises, you know I do. Tell me or you'll die hysterically."

"It's a really nice surprise Freddie, and if I keep squealing the neighbours will phone the police, again."

"Let them and I'll get you arrested for tormenting me."

He unleashed a barrage of little prods around the sides of her ribcage which got her almost frantic with laughter, tears streaming down her cheeks.

"Okay. Okay stop please, I'll tell you."

He reluctantly released her. The whole baby thing had created an increased seriousness to their relationship recently, but for today there had been a change, things had been a whole lot more fun again.

"You give up too easily, you chicken," he mocked.

"You were enjoying it too much, you bully."

He sat down on the sofa, slightly breathless.

She sat beside him, slightly coy.

"SO?" he demanded, holding a forefinger out ready to attack again.

"Okay, do you remember Chase?" she asked.

"Do I remember that pervert? I certainly do."

Just over a year previously a dance company had arrived to perform at THTC. They'd been accompanied by their recently commissioned costume designer, a young eccentric who lived locally to Swelford.

His name was Chase Everitts.

From their very first meeting, stage manager and costume designer had taken an instant dislike to each other.

There was something about Chase which didn't feel right to Freddie. He couldn't be exactly sure what it was, but for a start his refined Italian accent definitely sounded a bit dodgy.

Chase didn't like Freddie because he hadn't swooned over his self acclaimed fantastic costumes like many others had, and he was deeply offended by his lack of admiration.

Throughout rehearsals Freddie had found him lurking in the dark corners of the backstage area, hiding behind the drapes in the wings. It was all very creepy, and the young female dancers had vocalised some concerns about him as well.

So as soon as rehearsals were over and the performances were ready to begin Freddie had told Chase his job was done and he was no longer allowed to be backstage.

"I need to make sure everyone is dressed correctly," Chase pleaded. "My costumes are a statement of my importance to this production, they need to be perfect."

"You can check the costumes in the dressing rooms before they come up on stage," Freddie had insisted.

"But there are quick changes and I must be allowed access to supervise."

Chase's voice had almost reached fever pitch.

"Quick changes are just that chap, quick. The area is just big enough for the performers and there is no time for you to supervise."

"I demand to be allowed…"

He hadn't been given the chance to finish the sentence. Freddie had grabbed his arm and headed for the stage door.

"I've already checked with the performers and they say they don't need your help."

Two days later during the second show one of the female dancers came hurrying up to the SM's desk.

"There was someone leering at me in the quick change area."

"Any idea who it was, did you see him?" Freddie had asked.

"No but I saw a pair of pointy toed shoes under the cover drapes, and I think he's still there."

Freddie knew exactly who she was referring to.

He'd quickly swung off his chair and raced into the dark where he'd found Chase wrapped in one of the masking tabs, trying to hide.

"You have about a minute to get out of my theatre chap."

Freddie had grabbed hold of the back of his jacket and once again marched him to the stage door.

"Or what?" came the reply. The smooth Italian façade had suddenly disappeared, replaced by an angry and embarrassed Brummie spitting venom. "Oh the drama of it all. You're giving me a whole minute to get out of your theatre. Well boohoo, what then? Are you going to beat me up or something?"

"No, I'll just get you arrested for indecent exposure."

Freddie had pointed to where Chase, in his hurry and panic, had forgotten to tuck himself away.

"Although I don't think any of the witnesses will say they saw very much."

"Last time I saw him he was leaving with some kind of an excuse of a tail between his legs. So what's he got to do with this secret, nothing I hope."

"Well Oscar really likes his latest collection and thinks we should promote his work, after all he is a local lad."

"I'd heard his work was no longer desirable, well certainly not among the producers after they found out about his voyeuristic habits."

"Well, apparently he's developed a new range of lingerie and sleepwear, Oscar thinks it's good and worth a showing, he wants to set up a shoot."

Lisa was blushing again. "It's very skimpy and sexy, and Chase has promised to give me the range in my size to try out. I thought it might be a nice surprise for you."

Freddie looked thoughtful for a moment, then he raised his eyebrows and nodded his head slightly.

"I have to say I'm impressed."

"You'd better be or I'll run off with Oscar, he'll show me a good time."

"Oh there's no doubting you're fantastic and would look sexy in big white granny pants. But I meant I'm impressed with Chase."

"You sarcastic bugger," Lisa quipped. "Chase might be a degenerate but he's also a good designer."

"I'm not being sarcastic, I really am impressed

and I think he's really clever."

"But you haven't seen any of his designs yet."

"Don't need to, don't want to, but he's fast becoming a legend in my eyes."

"I don't understand, I thought you detested him."

"For what he did on my stage yes. But let's be honest here, every bloke in this world young or old, straight or gay, loves to look and feast their eyes on the beautiful, the sexy. Now you only become a pervert if you're caught doing it." He smiled as she stifled a laugh at this last line, he was right but it was unusual to hear a man admit it.

"Now it appears Chase has come up with a brilliant solution for his inability to be discreet. In the name of fashion he can dress pretty young girls in a way of his choosing and openly scrutinise them as his models, looking anywhere but in their eyes, and it will be perfectly acceptable and appropriate."

Freddie stood up and picked up his sandwich box from where he'd dropped it, "The guy's a genius and I'm actually impressed."

"It really couldn't be like that Freddie, surely he can't be that scheming and stupid. If he was caught he'd lose everything."

She was looking very thoughtful.

"Caught doing what? It's his collection, he has to make sure it's worn in the correct way and looks right. And you know how fussy designers are, picking at this, adjusting that, smoooothing."

He really emphasised this last word and let it hang.

"Well, must go," he said cheerily.

"Huh? Okay sorry yes, have a good show." She kissed him.

"Will you wait up," he already knew the answer.

"Probably not as we have to be awake again early tomorrow morning to make babies."

She was smiling again but he could see her mind was still elsewhere.

"With or without the big granny pants in the morning will be fine with me my sweet," he said and hurriedly left to avoid the magazine hurled in his direction.

As he pulled the door shut behind him he paused, he was sure he'd probably done enough and if nothing else had created some doubt. The light hadn't gone out in the hallway yet and he knew the lovely Lisa would be picking up the phone and dialling a number.

He wasn't being deliberately vindictive, although in his opinion the idiot didn't deserve another chance irrespective of how good he might be. But the fact remained that Chase really was 'that stupid' and could potentially create a serious problem for the people he really cared about. They had a lot more to lose than he did.

Was it really worth the risk for a few pairs of lacy pants?

"Hi Oscar, it's me," he heard. "I think we need to talk before we see Chase, I'll be with you in an hour."

Freddie smiled to himself and started to creep away.

"No, no problems. I'm just having second thoughts, that's all."

7.00 pm - The final performance of Oldklahoma.

Freddie was backstage and as there was no longer an atmosphere of doom he was sitting in his usual position at the control desk. The claustrophobic mood of negativity had long gone, replaced by a much livelier and friendly vibe. But as it was the last night the casts enthusiasm was slightly dampened by the disappointment of the approaching finale.

He reached for the switch marked 'Front of House' and turned it on.

"Good evening ladies and gentlemen and welcome to the Hidden Theatre Company for this evening's performance of Oldklahoma, brought to you by Swelford Amateur Musical Players. The house will open for you to take your seats in fifteen minutes. In the meantime why not consider avoiding the interval rush by pre-ordering your drinks at the bar. The curtain will rise for act one in thirty minutes, provided we can wake the cast from their pre-show nap, that's thirty minutes please, thank you."

Freddie turned 'Front of House' off and 'Back Stage' on. Once again it was time to rally the cast and crew, but tonight things were in total contrast for this final performance of the run compared to the start.

"This is your thirty minute call ladies and gentlemen, the house will open in fifteen minutes and so far ticket sales stand at...one hundred percent and there is a wait list for tonight's performance. All crew stations make your final checks and clear the stage. Thirty minutes stand-by please, Thirty minutes thank you."

As he switched the 'Back Stage' switch off he smiled to himself again, what a day, what a week. He set a timer for the fifteen minute call.

"Scotty?" he asked over his comms headset.

"Yes Boss," came the reply in his earpiece.

"Who's on coffee duty tonight?"

"I am Boss, I'm just in the process."

"As its last night, ask Arri in the bar if I can get a

little drop of magic please."

"No need boss I believe there's some heading your way as we speak."

Freddie heard footsteps approaching from behind and turned to see Alan the chairman walking toward him carrying a tumbler containing a rather large measure.

"The lads tell me you're partial to a drop of this." He held out the glass and Freddie took it."

"They make it sound like I'm an alcoholic but yes thanks, that's perfect."

"This is just to say thanks Freddie, personally from me, and there's a bottle of this behind the bar for you later. It's been a good show, eventually."

"My pleasure Alan, but to be honest you did it for yourselves, it just shows what a difference attitude can make. Oh and by the way the trustees have agreed to that discount we discussed."

"No need now Freddie, we've made that and more with the extra ticket sales, but thanks for that as well."

"I'm going to suggest you take it Alan, as it's been offered despite the fact they knew your income has improved over the past two nights. Treat it as a reward for the many years of loyalty to THTC."

"Then I accept, at least it'll keep us in the black at the bank for another year."

"Good news all round then, treat it as our sponsorship towards the next show. I take it you'll be able to keep going for another year now? We certainly hope so."

"Most definitely and we're going to build on your idea, if that's okay?"

"What idea?"

"Well we're going to look at show scripts we can do as ourselves, you know, keeping the 'old' theme you came up with. It's worked really well and I think with proper rehearsal time we can make more of it. The audience have obviously loved it and we've really enjoyed the challenge, well most of us have."

"Bob still not convinced?"

"Not really, he saying this is going to be his last show."

"Well I'm really surprised because he played the part well, but don't you dare tell him that. So what are you thinking of doing next year then?"

"It's not decided yet but surely you must have heard all the suggestions they've been discussing.. There a competition going on to see who can come up with the best idea."

"Like what? I haven't heard anything."

"The best one's so far include 'Granny get your gun', 'Pensioner on the roof' and 'Zimmering in the rain' but there are loads more."

Freddie was laughing so hard at this point that Steve interrupted him on the comms, "Move your mic please boss, we're all getting deafened."

"Sorry guys."

He did as he was asked and moved the boom arm of his headset away from his mouth, but everyone on comms were still able to listen in to the conversation through the open microphone.

"That's brilliant Alan, should work very well for you and I hope it does."

"Tell him Old Gits and Gals," Steve shouted in Freddie's earpiece.

"Thanks," Alan said. "But I want to ask you another big favour, something on behalf of the society."

"Whatever it is I can't afford it Alan," Freddie joked, his standard reply to any kind of request.

"Tell him Everything's Heading South Pacific." This time Scotty's was yelling in Freddie's earpiece.

"We were wondering if you would consider becoming our company director Freddie. We all know you well and respect your ideas, which have always been constructive and have helped us out immensely."

"Well I'm flattered Alan, really I am, but I just wouldn't have the time. This place is my world and is very possessive of my social life, in fact I don't have a social life. I just couldn't commit to any regular rehearsals."

"But because we're all retired we could rehearse anytime to suit you, day or night."

"Let me think about it..."

"Tell him I'll direct them," Steve shouted again in Freddie's earpiece. "And suggest they do 'The Widower of Oz'."

"Or how about 'Anything Goes but Nothing Works,'" Scotty shrieked with laughter.

"Just shut up for a minute will you," Freddie yelled.

"Okay, sorry Freddie, really sorry but I said I'd ask, thanks." Alan turned to go.

"Sorry, sorry not you Alan, everyone was talking at me through comms." He was pointing at his headset.

"Oh okay, no problem. I best get on, please think about my proposal Freddie."

"Can I add my suggestions for the next show?" Freddie called after him.

"Why not, after all, this 'old theme' was mainly your idea," the chairman replied."

"You better not be pinching any of our ideas Boss," Steve demanded in his ear.

"I fancy Jesus Christ Supernear or Grandmama Mia."

"Brilliant Freddie," Alan laughed. "Two definite contenders."

Freddie watched as the chairman walked away, his shoulders shaking uncontrollably. As he reached the stage door it sounded like he'd started sneezing.

"Seriously Boss?" Steve broke the silence over the comms. "Was that really the best you could come up with? I didn't get it."

"Well when you're older Steve, I guarantee you'll understand at least one of them."

10.20 pm - The final performance of 'Oldklahoma had received a standing ovation from the appreciative audience who'd sang lustily and laughed loudly throughout the entire show.

"At least Bob learned to control that scooter," Steve said to Freddie as they started the 'get-out' after the show.

"I'm just hoping the scenery company don't notice all the repairs to that fence and send us a bill."

"Did you hear there was a group of folk who came to Friday's show and rebooked for tonight? Told Ann it was the funniest thing they'd seen in years."

"I overheard someone asking Bob if 'The Full Monty' was available next year would he audition with or without the scooter," said Scotty.

"Bet he didn't find that funny at all."

"At least no one died this week," said Steve, "I was convinced somebody would keel over, especially that guy playing Jud."

"Well Claire was telling me that he was due to go into hospital to have a pacemaker fitted," Freddie said. "And he wanted to do one last show just in case. So you're right Steve, tragedy wasn't that far away."

"Talking of Claire, your Roy's really taken a shine to her," said Steve.

"Don't be daft, he only came in to check her out for a part in Panto."

"He's checked her out alright. I tell you he really likes that girl."

"She's the same age as me Steve. She's no more a girl than I'm a boy."

"You can be my boy Freddie," Brian said as he joined the conversation.

He always came backstage after the shows on the pretext of collecting discarded cups and glasses from the bar, but in reality he was always hoping for a bit of gossip, or a date.

"Sod off Brian, everyone's gone home," Freddie replied, "Anyway, why is it just lately I keep getting propositioned by gay men?"

"Because you're such a sweetie Freddie."

"It's true I am, but I'm not letting you treat me like one, I've seen you sucking mints Brian, no thanks, definitely not interested."

They all laughed.

"Anyway, I heard Steve mention your Uncle Roy, did you know he was in the audience again tonight?"

"Probably just having a second look at Claire."

"Why would he need a second look when he

signed her Wednesday night?"

"Never, he doesn't make quick decisions like that."

"He certainly did, and he's been here every show since then?"

"Has he?"

"And tonight he met her at the stage door with flowers."

"Did he?"

"Giggling like kids they were," Steve added.

"Were they?"

"Chauffeured limo outside as well, the works."

"That's rubbish Bri, Roy hates cars."

"He's trying to impress."

"Oh come on, you know what he's like. There isn't a female alive who could put up with his bizarre antics and unreasonable expectations."

"I know smitten when I see it."

"Well I'll guarantee that once she gets the full Roy treatment of habits and rituals she'll make a hasty dash for the door, or die of boredom."

"I bet she doesn't."

"Or he'll dump her the first time she drops her knickers on his immaculately hoovered floor, it'll all be over after a meal out together or the first time they jump into bed."

"I reckon they'll do both tonight," said Brian.

"Then they'll both be single again by this time tomorrow, which by the way will be the time we finish packing this show away if we don't get a move on. I'd like to make it home to my bed before one."

"And I bet your Uncle Roy's hoping for exactly the same."

Thirteen

December 2013

Sunday 8th 8.30 am. - Freddie was in the loading bay at THTC, supervising a handful of volunteers who were unloading the scenery for this week's stage production of Calendar Girls.

Only seven days of the early morning sex routine had passed so far and yet he looked completely and utterly knackered, and felt it too.

He'd been tenderly woken each and every morning at five thirty as Lisa had needed to spend extra time in the office to deal with a number of unexpected problems. While this was a good deal earlier than either of them had at first expected, Freddie had been surprisingly compliant. Despite the unwelcome disturbances to his slumbers he was determined not to let her down and had even managed to be quite chirpy and amenable, regardless of the fact he felt like a zombie on tranquilizers.

The sex had been basic and mechanical rather

than intimate, but Lisa was satisfied that her revised routine was going well. There was no doubt that her willing hubbie had made a concerted effort, for which she'd been really grateful, and she'd made a million promises to make it up to him.

But his valiant attempts to fulfil her maternal desire were coming at a cost. His energy levels had plummeted and as each day passed he was experiencing an increased weariness that wasn't just about the early mornings, it was more because he wasn't sleeping properly.

Sex at night had nearly always resulted in Freddie becoming immediately comatose, unlike sex in the morning which was having the opposite effect completely, and by the time Lisa had gone to work at seven he would be wide awake.

He wanted to go back to sleep but couldn't, and was unable to nap during the day either, which had never been a problem before.

At night he'd finally manage to enter the 'land of nod' around three in the morning, and only then after he'd sneaked a couple of large single malts from a bottle he had hidden in the kitchen.

An overly busy work schedule wasn't helping the situation either.

Freddie, Steve and Scotty mainly worked evenings and weekends, as is the general nature of the entertainment industry. But as the only paid technical staff they were also required to be available at all other times to meet the needs of the business, and more recently things were getting hectic.

The past week had been one of these times.

The Sunday immediately after Oklahoma the whole team had been in early to get everything ready for a three day holiday industry conference. Each day, at nine o'clock in the morning, a new batch of a hundred or so fresh-faced and happy Travel Agents from the south of England duly poured out of the nearby hotel and into the venue. There were talks and workshops throughout the day followed by a two hour cabaret to amuse each group in the evenings.

In four days Freddie had clocked up fifty eight hours.

Then he was in again early Thursday morning, the day after the conference, to clear up and get everywhere ready and set-up for the next customers. The smaller performance area, known as 'The Cube', was hosting an open mic night that evening, and a Comedy Roadshow was on stage in the 'Main House' Friday and Saturday.

It wasn't always arduous for the staff but they often worked very long and tiring hours. Such a crazy schedule wasn't normally an issue, but this particularly demanding period couldn't have come at a worse time for Freddie.

Unsurprisingly, with everything that was going on, he was losing control of an invigorated worry monkey which was edging its way back into his thoughts, lurking and growing as it fed on the negativity bought on by fatigue.

....'*Just how long can you keep this up? I've never known you this tired'*....it mocked.

"Sod off monkey," he mumbled.

"You okay Boss?"

Freddie had been in his own little world and had forgotten he was helping Steve to carry a large table off the tailgate of the scenery lorry and into the scenery dock.

"Err, yes sorry Steve. Just need a moment."

He slumped down in the old armchair near the door.

Steve tossed his eye and headed back to the lorry to collect more furniture.

Freddie picked up the nearby mug of lukewarm coffee and took a big slurp, then put it down again.

....*'What if it's another unsuccessful month?*....

Freddie felt thoroughly dejected and sat staring into space.

....*'How long do you think you can keep this up?'*....

"As long as it takes monkey," he muttered under his breath. "Why don't you just bugger off."

....*'You better hope she doesn't find that bottle'*....

He lifted his coffee mug but paused with the rim just under his nose.

....*'She'll kill you if she finds it'*....

He sat upright with a sudden realisation,

"Oh shit," he cursed. "I've completely forgotten about that pot. She's more likely to kill me if she finds that."

"What pot's that then Boss?"

Steve had returned carrying two chairs and was looking quizzical.

"Sorry?" Freddie enquired putting his mug down.

"You just said you'd forgotten about that pot."

"Did I really say that out loud?"

"Well you've been wittering all morning, which isn't unusual for you, but you normally make a bit more sense. What's all this about monkeys and pots and how long can you keep it going?"

"I'm just really tired is all Steve."

"Aren't we all? That conference last week was a killer, and what's coming isn't going to be any better either." Steve put the chairs down and sat on one.

"Why did they have to book out the Cube during the day for the whole of next week? After all it's only a schools drama showcase and they knew we had this big show going on as well?"

"Regular customers Steve, and we need the money. It's a nuisance, but let's just get through this week and after that things should be quieter for a while, and hopefully better."

"Quieter and better? With the pantomime get-in and fit-up the day after we take this one out, you're having a laugh Boss?"

"It won't be too bad this year I promise. The set isn't that big and Roy always finds plenty of willing volunteers. Once everything is set up and running it'll be six easy weeks of evenings only."

"I still think they've got a cheek piling the work up like they do."

"It keeps us in a job mate. That's the reality. Come on, look on the bright side, at least you're getting paid the overtime, I get zip for all the extra time I put in and still have to pay tax on that."

Steve laughed.

"Why don't you go home for a couple of hours Boss, me and Scotty can handle the fit-up."

"I know you could mate, and thanks for the offer. But Lisa's not at home and if I did get to sleep I may never wake up again, ever. But I will go and have a lie down for an hour before the run through if that's okay."

There was a large comfy pile of old black cloth drapes in the props cupboard they all used when

173

there was spare time to take a well earned break.

"I don't know how you can lie down on those old blacks Boss."

Steve screwed his face up in disgust, "I wouldn't go anywhere near them knowing what Brian gets up to in there."

"You mean what he's tried to get up to in there. To my knowledge nothing has ever happened, except for his attempt to burn this place down."

He gave his fly captain a smile, raised his eyebrows and nodded in a direction over Steve's shoulder. Scotty was coming and saw the gesture.

"Don't bother about me," Scotty announced sitting down on the other chair.

"Steve's already told me all the sordid details of Brian's escapades in the props cupboard. You don't need to protect me from all the filth and debauchery that goes on around here Boss, I'm becoming immune to it."

That raised a chuckle.

Scotty's unique sense of humour was developing into a great asset for keeping them all cheery, despite their tiredness.

"Talking of debauchery," Freddie said. "The cast are in at twelve, have you finished plotting the lighting yet young 'un?"

"All done except for the specials. It shouldn't take me long once I know where they'll be standing. When do they want to start?"

"They want to run through the calendar photo shoot scenes first to make sure everything's set-up in the right place, they don't want any intimate body bits to be seen by the audience."

"So is what Steve's been saying true then?"

Scotty suddenly sounded anxious.

"Are we seriously going to have fully naked ladies on the stage?"

"It's Calendar Girls mate," Steve insisted.

"The whole show is dependent on the fact that the ladies from the WI pose nude for a calendar shoot to raise money for charity."

"Yes, yes, I know the story, but I thought they'd be covering certain bits up with body stockings or something. I didn't think they'd be flashing their wobbly bits on an open stage for everyone to see."

"The views could be terrific," Steve said with a wink.

"They're certainly a lot younger than SAMPS," Freddie added. "And they've managed to find some new talent locally especially for this production."

"Oh cheers Boss, knowing they live round here makes me feel so much better," Scotty said sarcastically.

Now I have to deal with the prospect of seeing Miss July next time I'm in McD's, watching her eat a sodding fillet o'fish with the image of her naked body burnt into my innocent brain. Or how about bumping into Miss September when I'm out shopping with my grandmother. How embarrassing will that be?"

Freddie and Steve smiled.

Scotty had a reputation for feeling awkward around nudity and was becoming famous for his 'I'm too young for all this' rants, which in full flow were exceptionally funny.

"Can't you just imagine the scenario, I'm at Tesco's checkout with my Gran on a Thursday afternoon and the lady in front of us is placing her fruit and veg onto the conveyer. She spots me waiting in line right behind her.

'Hello Scotty' she says. *'Fancy seeing you in here'*

'Erm, Hi Miss September' I reply with a polite smile as my Gran tugs at my elbow.

'Scotty' Gran says, *'Aren't you going to introduce me to you friend?'*

'Of course Gran' I reply. *'This is Miss September, she has perky tits, but she's not really a natural blonde'*

'Oh that's nice dear' Gran says, *'And how do you know that?'*

So now in the middle of Tesco's surrounded by hundreds of people and my wonderfully caring, slightly deaf, god-fearing grandmother, I announce to the whole world,

'Because I've seen her ginger bush Gran.'

He paused and sighed.

"I'm far too young for my sexual fantasies about women to be dominated by images of mature women."

If he was expecting a bit of sympathy or support, there was none. Steve and Freddie just sat there and stared at him, their faces showing no emotion.

"What is it with you two?" he whined. "Aren't you even slightly uncomfortable about the situation? If any of them were relatives of mine I certainly wouldn't want the public staring at their pubics."

Freddie laughed.

"The audience don't get to see anything Scotty," he reassured. "A clever use of scenery and props keeps the ladies modesty covered. It's not going to be a flesh fest for all the local voyeurs you know, well at least I hope it's not going to be like that."

He looked at Steve, "Please tell me all your

strange mates from the fishing club aren't going to turn up here this week Steve."

Steve ignored him.

"So why do they have to take everything off if no one's going to see anything," Scotty protested.

"Because the audience have to believe that the ladies are really naked. The best way to do that is for them to actually be naked. Its far better they accidentally show a nipple rather than a bra strap."

"It's not what the audience might see that worries me." Scotty sounded genuinely flustered.

"Yes, you're absolutely right mate," Steve exclaimed. "The props will only cover the view from the front. Can you imagine what will be on display for all of us to see from the wings?"

"I don't want to. Please Boss, can I work up in the control room, away from it all?"

"You're down to be ASM and co-ordinate the volunteers organising the props backstage."

"Aw Boss, no," he simpered as he put his chin on his chest and folded his arms in a sulk.

Freddie and Steve could contain themselves no longer and erupted into heaving fits of hysterics.

Scotty wasn't impressed.

"Oh I get it, it must be wind-up the youngster season again. Very funny people."

"Don't worry lad," Freddie said, wiping his eyes with the back of his hand. "There's going to be a briefing after the rehearsals. As soon as the stage is set for each scene the plan is to clear the backstage area of all men, even their partners."

"But not you though Boss?" Steve said with a grin.

"Trust me Steve, I'll definitely be watching the

front of house monitors and nothing else. As for you lad, you'll be able to run away and hide, somewhere out of sight. Just stay on comms."

"Grateful Boss, really I am."

"Joking aside, just remember both of you, the ladies in this production have probably never stripped off for anyone other than their partners before now. They'll almost certainly feel worse showing it than you do looking at it. If you're going to make a career of this then you'll have to get used to lots of unusual people in various states of undress, that's totally unavoidable. A laugh and a joke between us is okay, but face to face we all have to remain professional. Okay?"

"Okay," the other two said in unison.

Freddie suddenly jumped to his feet.

"So back in the real world I think we should get on."

He pushed his mug towards the youngster.

"Coffee all round lad and make the driver one as well please."

That light interlude had worked well to distract his monkey for a while.

"And if I were you pair," he added as he put on his gloves ready for action. "I'd try to remember that all the volunteers this week are the husbands and family of the women getting their kit off. So it's probably not a good idea to go around making jokes about the views. As I said before let's just get through this week, with our sanity still intact if possible."

He headed back out to the wagon.

"And if all else fails," he called back to them.

"Shut your eyes."

Fourteen

Thursday 12th 11.32 am - Freddie gradually opened his eyes and felt an immediate and growing chill of disappointment.

His dream had been a wonderful warm moment of peace and harmony in total contrast to his current awakening state, now he felt miserably cold and very much alone.

He'd been walking with the lovely Lisa by the river, a familiar and often visited place of their early days together. With the heat of the sun on his face, the smell of meadow grass under his feet and the soft touch of her hand in his he'd felt genuine contentment. Overwhelmed by an intense sense of belonging he knew he'd been in the place he wanted to be, with the person he wanted to be with, and she was happy and carefree.

It had been a proper dream, one which had made him feel all warm and fuzzy inside, a timeless memory of perfection, a reminder of the blissful joy of togetherness and a futile grasp at a desire for the way things were before reckless abandon had been kicked to death by obsessive need.

As the fragmented remains of the dream cleared, positive emotions were rapidly being replaced by the harshness of an increasingly hollow reality, his bleary eyes focused on the unerring reminder of his anxiety. That damn sample pot was sitting in full view on his bedside table with a shaft of sunlight shining directly onto it through the curtains.

Suddenly panic set in, why had he left it there?

If Lisa saw it and realised it was still empty after nearly three weeks then...

"Hang on a minute," he said quietly to himself. "Something is definitely wrong."

The pot had been buried deep at the back of the drawer and he certainly hadn't taken it out, so who had?'

Maybe she'd found it and left it there for him to see, loudly declaring that she was on to him, fully aware of his laziness. He tried to sneak a glance over his shoulder, was she behind him in the bed, waiting for him to wake and listen to his pathetic excuses.

He slowly moved his foot back and felt it brush against something warm. She was there alright, and now his touch had disturbed her, he could feel her stirring.

He had to hide that pot.

He reached out to the handle of the drawer as carefully as he could and gently pulled on it, desperate not to let her know he was awake. But the drawer was shut tight as if glued in defiance, willing him to be found out it refused to budge. So he pulled harder and harder.

As he felt her grab his shoulder and gently shake

it he started to shout.

"Open up damn you, what have I done in my life to deserve this? Please you must let me in, you must let me have one day more."

"Oh if only you'd say that to me when you're awake Freddie my boy."

Freddie stopped tugging at the stubborn drawer as the unseen hand continued to shake his shoulder. And why was Brian's voice suddenly in his head?

"Come on Freddie, wakey wakey. Roy's here to see you."

He sat bolt upright and this time he opened his eyes properly and saw true reality.

He wasn't in bed with the lovely Lisa, tormented by his plastic nemesis revealed as he'd thought, he was sitting in the auditorium of THTC as Brian gently shook him from his slumbers.

"I dreamed a dream," Freddie said to his friend.

"Were there castles on a cloud and lovely ladies?" Brian asked playing the game.

"Not really, but at the end of the day who am I?" Freddie sighed.

"You're a miserable git Freddie, now go and swill your face, Roy's in the office."

"Hello Uncle, this is a nice surprise."

Roy looked worried. He gave a really deep and heavy sigh.

"Look son, it's come to my attention that I've been a bit neglectful of my duties toward you."

"I can't say I understand what you're talking about Roy, but you've been anything but neglectful."

"Thank you for saying that, but there's something you need to know."

"Oh is this the bit where you tell me all about Claire and how she's made you the happiest..."

"Time for a bit of serious lad, please."

Freddie could see his uncle meant it.

"But it has got something to do with Claire, yes, well more because of Claire really," Roy added.

"I heard you two were getting on well."

"Very well lad. I'm very fond of her."

"I'm pleased for you, but this isn't a surprise Uncle. They were all talking about you at THTC, so I already knew."

"That's not what I came to tell you lad."

"Oh, sorry. Go on then."

Freddie was starting to worry about Roy, he was the only relative he had left and hoped he wasn't about to reveal he was sick.

"Well we were chatting last night and we were doing the 'revealing our past' bit. She told me she has two grown lads, then asked if I had and children."

"Which you don't."

"Because I can't Freddie."

"Because you've never been in a serious relationship before?"

"Because I'm sterile lad."

Uncle and nephew just sat looking at each other. Freddie was wondering why Roy had felt it necessary to make a special visit to the theatre to divulge this very personal bit of information.

"Sorry to hear that Roy, but not wanting to be insensitive, does it really matter at your age?"

Roy cleared his throat, took a drink of the coffee Ann had made him, then cleared his throat again.

"The men in our family have always had a bit of a problem when it comes to producing children

Freddie. There's a..."

He hesitated and took another gulp of coffee.

"There's a genetic problem in our family Freddie, passed down from father to son. It's not something that's going to shorten your life, but it can cause certain...certain fertility problems."

"Like what?"

"Well it varies. Your mom and dad had been trying desperately for many years before you came along and, as I remember things, they were hoping for more, but it never happened."

"So you're saying that might explain why Lisa's not pregnant yet, I may have the same condition."

"Afraid so lad, in fact it's highly likely."

"But as I came along eventually it seems that everything worked okay for dad, just slowly."

"It varies son, like I said, I'm completely sterile."

"Oh...I see."

For just a brief moment Freddie was busy fending off his annoying little worry monkey who'd suddenly emerged from the shadows where it had been waiting for an opportunity to strike.

....*'There you go then Freddie'*....it taunted.

....*'that'll teach you to ignore me, you can't give the lovely Lisa exactly what she wants, and without a baby you're finished, just a barren joke'*....

With all his emotional strength Freddie lashed out and dismissed the repulsive creature.

"But you don't know for sure if I'm affected," he yelled loudly.

The eruption took Roy by surprise.

"I'm really sorry Roy," Freddie said apologetically.

"I didn't mean to shout like that."

He was just grateful he hadn't added 'you hideous little shit' which was exactly what was in his mind to shout at monkey.

"No it's okay son, I understand you're upset."

Uncle Roy stood up and placed a warming hand on his nephews shoulder.

"And the answer to that question is no I don't know. The doctor told me that it was something to do with an extra chromosome, a genetic problem that would almost certainly be passed on to affect every male member of the family. I'm sorry son."

"Don't be Uncle, and thanks for telling me."

"I should have done it sooner."

"Maybe it's a secret we both need to keep...for now."

Fifteen

Saturday 14th 15.10 pm - For the last few minutes Brian and Ann had been busily scanning the eight small CCTV monitors in the box office.

Freddie was missing, and searching the many different areas of the theatre for clues as to his whereabouts was far easier from here than trudging aimlessly around the building.

They knew he'd wandered off somewhere to fetch some required piece of equipment, but in the process he'd obviously found a hiding place, again

For the last two days Freddie's usual persona had dramatically altered. He'd become moody, and short tempered, but more significantly he kept disappearing for hours on end.

For the umpteenth time that week the office staff were on 'Freddie Watch', and they were really worried about him.

"He's been gone nearly an hour," Ann said. "Where can he have got to?"

"I'll go up to the Cave," Brian said pointing at

one of the screens,

"Look, it's too dark in there to see anything and I reckon that's where he'll be hiding. Make some strong coffee and cut that lovely cake you've made and I'll go and see if I'm right. We need to get him organised before tonight's show."

Freddie was struggling.

His tattered emotions had been laid bare, and as well as being tired, he felt incredibly unhappy. As Brian had suspected he was sat brooding in the darkness of the Cave, but he wasn't asleep.

Freddie's little worry monkey had been allowed to freely poke around in his head since Roy's visit. With irritating little fingers it was opening up perceived cracks in his relationship, damaging the softening edges of their once firm love for each other, or so he thought. His increasingly fatigued mind was allowing too many seeds of doubt to quickly germinate and grow into large bushes of discontentment and uncertainty, and he was just too tired to fight back.

The door to the Cave cracked open and an unwelcome shaft of light fell in.

"You better have coffee and cake Brian," Freddie said.

"Not on me, but Ann is sorting it out right now. You coming?"

Brian switched the lights on and saw his friend wince and turn his glum face away from the brightness.

"I bet you can't guess how many hours I've spent with Lisa in the past two weeks."

"I know it's been tough my boy, but...."

"Three hours mate, three hours that's all. And

what did we do in those one hundred and eighty minutes? Well we spent most of that time trying to make a baby and the rest just yawning at each other."

"Making babies sounds good fun, I suppose, if you like that sort of thing."

"I used to."

Brian came into the room and sat in the chair next to his friend.

"We haven't eaten together, slept together or even had an argument together. I'm no longer a real person I'm just a means to an end...and right at this moment that's in question. I'm only thirty six and can honestly say I'm sick of sex."

"And the moment will pass and everything will get back to normal soon."

"Convince me."

"Look, I know someone who's advice would be to stop sulking because it doesn't change anything and only serves to poison your mind. Good advice if you ask me."

"Well that's just stupid."

"Then you're stupid, because that's what you told me when I found out Ashley, that gorgeous dancer from Roy's company, had been playing me for a fool for six months."

"Oh come on, that was totally different, you two were never going..."

"Why was that so different you selfish little shit?"

Brian turned away, his voice softened to a whisper.

"Just because it seemed petty nonsense to you doesn't mean it was trivial and meaningless for me."

Freddie cringed at the realisation of his own reckless and less than thoughtful remark. He couldn't think of anything to say in his own defence, probably because he knew Brian was absolutely right and he'd been such a knob.

"You're right Bri, I'm sorry," Freddie said.

"That would be exactly what I'd say, in fact I've probably said it a lot more often than once. I know I'm being a pain, but I've never felt this far away from Lisa before and it hurts."

Brian turned back to face him with a big soppy grin on his face.

"I know it does," he said.

"And the time will come when all of this will be forgotten and the two of you will be just as you were before, trust me. You're always telling everyone to stop letting the worry monkeys lie to them. I suggest you should take your own advice and stop blowing it all out of proportion."

"I wish I could and I also wish I hadn't upset you. I'm a right idiot."

"And a selfish little shit."

"Yes I am, and I'm really sorry I suggested your infatuation with empty headed Ashley, the chisel chinned prancer, was any less important than...hang on a minute, you despised that bloke."

"Did I?"

"The first time you went out together he demanded money off you."

"Did he?"

"It didn't last six hours let alone six months, he was playing you, just like you're doing to me right now."

"Yes I am, and it worked. See I've got you smiling again."

"You do this every time. You a good friend Bri, a

friend I don't deserve sometimes."

"That's true you don't, now snap out of it and give me a hug."

"Brian."

"We're family Freddie and we should look out for each other."

They both stood and embraced like long lost brothers.

"Brian?" Freddie said, "I'm not sure real family would be feeling my bum at a time like this."

"We're a very close family Freddie my darling boy. Very, very close."

Sixteen

Tuesday 17th 5.40 a.m. - Lisa crept into the spare room carrying two steaming mugs of herbal tea and placed them down on the bedside table.

Having showered and laid out her clothes for the day, she now took off her dressing gown and slid effortlessly under the duvet to lie naked beside a gently snoring Freddie.

She felt guilty about having to disturb her hard working hubby every morning, especially as for the last two weeks he'd insisted on sleeping in the spare room so as not to disturb her when he came to bed late. Even so, she was keen to keep the routine going and was sure everything would work out for the best, sooner rather than later.

As usual she had a lot going on at work today and couldn't delay waking him up any longer. She gently shook his shoulder.

A tuft of tousled hair sticking out from under the edge of the duvet twitched, and as signs of life began to emerge a bout of furious scratching started.

"Wake up sleepy head, I need to be in early again, sorry."

A bleary eyed Freddie appeared from under the duvet.

"So you need me to get in early as well then, don't you?" Freddie joked.

He'd decided for now not to tell her about 'the problem' and carry on as normal. That hadn't been an easy decision to make because in reality he was terrified she'd find out accidentally. But then without any proof he had the condition the uncertainty it would cause if he told her could be devastating.

He needed to fill that pot and find out one way or the other.

"You should go for a nice long walk this morning, it'll clear your head," Lisa was saying.

"What now?"

"No, when we're finished silly."

"I thought I might try to get back to sleep. I didn't get to bed until three."

"And I'm just saying a bit more exercise wouldn't hurt sweetie. Aren't you ready yet?"

"Well at this precise moment I'm doing my best. If you're in a rush then maybe you could do something to help my flagging resolve."

"Always the joker Freddie, come on, hurry up."

She reached over and grabbed his penis and started tugging at it roughly.

"Hey, not so heavy handed," he yelped.

Then, even less gently, she pulled him on top of her.

"Let's get going and I won't have to hurt you again," she said brightly trying to lighten the situation.

She really hadn't meant to be this sharp with him, but she was tired as well and had her own problems working to impossible deadlines.

"Resorting to threats now are we?"

"Stop talking and hurry up please sweetie."

"I'm sorry," he said rolling off her and onto his back. "You're going to have to fuel my desire, kindle my fire and excite my ardour."

"What are you talking about you crazy man?"

"I thought that might be a bit obvious by the fact I'm not erect yet. I need some encouragement."

"Oh you've got to be kidding me Freddie, I really don't have time for your games. Are you deliberately being difficult?"

"Look I'm sorry but I'm just so shattered I'm obviously not in the mood."

"Isn't that my line?"

"Well it may be your line, but unless we can get it working then I can't do anything with it."

"You mean to tell me you've got absolutely no control over it?"

"You have more control over it than me, so may I suggest if you want it now you'll need to do something to resolve the situation."

She threw back the duvet with a grump to reveal her naked body. Inelegantly she opened her legs wide and at the same time grabbed the head of his penis, squeezing it a few times, but again none too gently.

"There, is that enough to wake the dead," she said coldly. "I really am on a deadline here Freddie so a little bit of cooperation wouldn't go amiss."

"Well it appears you're an expert at milking cows but that's about as stimulating as smacking it with a brick."

"Now there's an idea. Just hurry up will you, I'm getting cold."

"And impatient, give me chance."

What was wrong with him, this had never happened before.

"I don't have time for you to mess around like this Freddie." She was starting to sound irritated.

"I'm sorry, but this feels like the early morning equivalent of 'pull my nightie down when you've finished' type of sex. You're not really in the room are you, so how come you expect me to be. Can't we give it a miss for now and maybe you could come back later on, when I'm..."

"It has to be now Freddie," she protested.

"Well you only said it had to be in the morning and it'll still be morning for another six hours yet."

"Stop being pedantic and hurry up, you're just being deliberately awkward."

"Why would I do that? Maybe you just need to accept that for once I don't fancy doing it. If I'm being honest it's no longer any fun."

He jumped off the bed grabbed her dressing gown and tried to put it on.

"This is just regimented make babies sex. I'm sorry but I can't perform on demand this morning."

"You missed the word 'try' Freddie, try to make baby sex, there'll be no baby unless we keep trying." Her voice had become harsh, the earlier softer tone had vanished.

"Sarcastic bullying doesn't create an atmosphere for intimacy and if we can't be intimate I can't do it," he replied. He threw her robe back on the bed and went hunting for his.

"That's so typical of a man," she shouted.

"If the woman doesn't want sex you men sulk and moan about how it's only natural to get aroused around such a sexy lady. You bitch and whinge until you get what you want. But if a woman wants sex, suddenly IT doesn't work and that's the end of the matter. That's pathetic Freddie."

"I'm sorry about this, really I am, but I'm not a young man anymore you know, and the way you've been abusing me lately I'd be surprised if I have anything left that isn't as knackered as the rest of me. We used to take our time, we made love, but now I've just become a sperm donor."

"Maybe if your donations were a bit more generous in content you wouldn't need to give as often. And I haven't abused you, as you claim, you've been abusing yourself. I know all about the whiskey in the kitchen cupboard Freddie, two bottles in three weeks, no wonder you can't get me pregnant, you fill your body full of shit instead of taking care of it."

"There's nothing wrong with me."

"So when are we going to find that out for sure then?" she demanded.

"Find out what?"

"When did the clinic say the results would be ready?

"Oh...well..."

Now he was in trouble.

"Oh Freddie, don't tell me you forgot to ask how long the tests would take."

There could never be any reason for him to lie to her, he'd just have to admit it. But he didn't get the chance to say anything, she knew by his body language.

"You haven't done it have you."

"No, and there's no point in offering an excuse, you won't listen."

"Try me."

"I was just too tired, too busy, pick a reason."

"You were right, I'm not listening."

She was shouting again.

"You're sodding useless."

"This is not my fault," he shouted back.

"There's only the two us involved in this Freddie."

Her voice was starting to break up with emotion.

"It doesn't take a genius to figure out that one of us must be faulty."

That maybe be closer to the truth than she realises, Freddie was thinking.

"Please Lisa, don't do this. Even if one of us is faulty, as you put it, it's not deliberate it's unfortunate. I'm sure everything will be fine, we just need time."

"You haven't even bothered to fill that pot so we can find out."

She was furious.

"You have all day on your own," she screamed.

"But as usual if it's not what selfish Freddie wants then it doesn't get done, right?"

"That's unfair. I've always done what you want me to do, and I've always wanted what you want."

"Then prove it now. I want a baby."

"I know you do, but all this anger doesn't help."

"I want a baby and it's going to happen with or without your help."

She turned her back, bounced out of the room

and slammed the door. He heard the sobbing start just before the other bedroom door crashed into its frame.

This was no longer casual innuendo combined with playful teasing, this was serious.

Their bedroom had finally become a battlefield, it was literally 'load up and charge' but in the heat of this conflict Freddie was out of ammunition and the ensuing fight had dared to question the ownership and quality of the gun.

His immediate instinct was to follow her but he hesitated, the realisation of what she'd just said was slowly sinking in.

He sat back down on the bed, his shoulders slumped, his mind awhirl, torn between wanting to hold the love of his life but haunted by the suggestion of betrayal that same love had just made.

He heard her come out of the bedroom, clatter down the stairs and out of the front door a few seconds later, yet another door to slam.

His worry monkey came hurtling back, only this time it had good reason to gatecrash his thoughts.

.....'Now you're really in trouble'.....

Monkey took a firmer grip, it had more than a foot in the door this time.

Freddie was desperate to dispel his anxiety.

"She only said those things out of anger and frustration, she didn't mean it."

.....'Why did she say it if she didn't mean it?'.....

His future with the lovely Lisa was disappearing, with the hand of that damn worry monkey pulling at the plug to empty out his dreams.

But he wasn't beaten yet, this dream was worth fighting for.

He just needed a plan

...."There's nothing you can do to put this right"....

"I know your game monkey," he murmured. "You're a dark and sinister creature with no sense of right or wrong. But your lies won't destroy me monkey, that's never going to happen."

.....'I haven't told a single lie'.....

He needed to rid himself of the demons lurking in the dark corners of his mind before they got a hold. Quickly throwing on his clothes he headed downstairs and made himself a cup of tea.

'Always the right thing to do in a crisis' he thought.

Wandering into the living room he slumped down on the sofa. For once the silence he loved was oppressive, he felt truly dejected and utterly alone.

"...and after the break we'll be talking to a lovely young lady who says her boyfriend of twenty years is denying being the father of their eighteen year old daughter. DNA results on the Aven Davis show after the break. Don't miss it."

With all that had happened Freddie couldn't believe he'd switched the TV on, but now it had got his attention.

It felt relevant.

He refused to believe that Lisa's comment meant she'd actually consider involving another man as an option to their problem. But after months without success, how would he react now if in the next few weeks she sudden declared she was pregnant?

Even worse as Roy had suggested there might be a problem.

With this thought Freddie's shoulders dropped

again, a hollow sinking feeling was gnawing in his chest.

He'd never considered there was anything that could spoil his life with Lisa, their love for each other, their happiness.

"...It could be the pressure of work or an underlying medical problem, but one in four men over the age of 40 suffer from occasional erectile dysfunction. Your GP can help."

"Bloody hell, that's spooky," he shouted at the TV. "But you missed out 'Completely knackered owing to an overly broody wife."

"That's it," he said.

"She can't help the way she's acting, its instinct. In the wild she would have ditched this failing male ages ago and found herself a young healthy, virile stud. That wasn't my lovely Lisa, it was some hideously hormone soaked monster desperate to breed."

He snapped straight out of his mood and knew exactly what he should do.

He was frantically searching for the remote.

"We've never been like this before, so far apart and fighting. This has to be sorted out right now or the consequences could destroy what we've got, what I've got. I'll phone her first and apologise."

"...and welcome back to the Aven Davis show…"

"You're not welcome Aven, you're a killer of hope and dreams. You take the innocent, rip out their very soul and kick it to death on national television, and all in the name of entertainment."

"...so let's hear her side of the story first..."

"Or not," said Freddie.

The remote had been discovered behind a cushion.

"...Please welcome Karen to the show."

Freddie's thumb pushed down on the 'off' button.

He couldn't afford to waste another second thinking about other people's problems, he had to do something about his own.

Racing over to the phone he dialled her office number.

Surely their relationship was strong, he just had to be honest.

"Honey, please listen, I'm so sorry, really I am. I know I've let you down but we can't...."

"You haven't let anyone down Freddie darling."

It wasn't Lisa.

"Oscar?"

"Sorry Freddie, she's just stepped out for a while."

"Is she okay?"

"I don't give a shit to be honest Freddie darling, and I've told her exactly that and a few other home truths as well. I hope she's sobbing herself hoarse as we speak."

"What?"

"Don't get me wrong, I love her like the daughter I never wanted. But lately she's become a selfish grump. Bouncing into the office like she did, slamming doors and bad mouthing you my precious boy."

"But it's all my fault Oscar, I'm totally to blame for upsetting her like that."

"Well that's right Freddie you are, and you're also talking a load of bollocks."

"I haven't got a clue what you're talking about Oscar, speak English."

"Look Freddie darling, it is your fault that she's gone off on one, yes. But it's not because you couldn't get it up this morning, oh no, and not because she's not pregnant yet, oh no no. This is all your Freddie fault because you've spent the last twenty years treating her like a goddess."

"She's told everyone that I couldn't....oh great."

"Only most of the people in earshot of a nuclear explosion, so not that many really. But be quiet and let me finish what you need to hear my boy."

Freddie did as he was told, Oscar was not one to argue with.

"She certainly has no right or reason to treat you like she did Freddie darling, but she's so used to you doing anything to keep her happy that she reacted like the overindulged bitch you've created her to be."

"Oh come on Oscar, she's not like that at all."

"She's not like that normally, you meant to say my boy. Normally she always gets what she wants from you. Normally you fulfil her every desire. Normally she's contented because you don't give her any grief...do you Freddie?"

"No, but that's what makes me happy, doing what she wants."

"So it maybe my boy, but I have to ask is it really a good idea to let someone have her own way all of the time. It stops them from realising that you actually have an opinion and the right to do your own thing. Tell her no occasionally, otherwise...oh hang on a minute, she's back and she looks like shit. I'll put her on, but don't you dare apologise."

He heard muffled voices exchanging words.

"Oscar's right."

Her voice sounded weak and timid.

"I don't deserve you Freddie and as much as I want this baby, I can't be without you. I'm so very sorry about this morning, about every morning."

"I can't imagine my life without you either. Let's just blame over enthusiastic natural instincts and forget about this morning."

"You're such a sweetie Freddie."

"I hope you still think that when I tell you there might be a problem after all...with me."

"Like what?"

He took a deep breath, this was going to be painful.

"Roy told me the other day that he's sterile and he thinks it might run in the family."

There was no reply, just silence for what seemed like ages.

Then she started to cry softly.

"I'm really sorry I wasn't thinking clearly, I should have told you I know, I just didn't want to hurt you."

"You haven't hurt me Freddie."

Her voice was breaking up with emotion.

"I'm upset with myself for what I've put you through, instead of being a better friend. You must have been worried sick."

"The only thing that matters to me is that you still want to be with me."

"Of course I do silly, it's always been you, even

before it was you it was you. I want us and us can never be less than two."

"You don't know how happy that makes me."

He stuck two fingers up to his monkey.

....*'It's not over yet Freddie, what about the problem?...*

"Then I'll have to find out for sure if we can be three," he said aloud.

"You don't have too sweetie," Lisa replied, not realising he wasn't speaking to her.

"If you'd rather not know I'm okay with that."

Lisa sounded much happier now.

"No, I need to know...we need to know. I'm off to fill that pot now...as long as it's not going to upset you if I waste a few?"

"No not at all. Tell you what, how about some phone sex to help you out."

"Well I'll not say no to that. Seriously?"

"You go and fetch the pot while I get rid of you know who."

Excitedly Freddie sprang up the stairs two at a time still with the phone in his hand. Barging into the bedroom he opened his bedside drawer and grabbed the small plastic tormentor, the insignificant object that had caused him so much anguish over the last couple of weeks.

Sitting down on the bed he wasn't quite sure now if this was such a good idea. As thrilling as it had initially seemed, he now felt a little awkward.

He put the phone back to his ear.

"On second thoughts," he said, "Maybe, I should just do this on my own."

There was some stifled giggling in the back ground.

"Oh I get it," he laughed.

"You were just teasing and we're back to normal again. I bet I'm on speaker phone as well, yes? Come on tell me the truth, who's there?"

There were a few muffled sounds and more sniggering.

"Hello again Freddie darling."

It was Oscar.

"Hazel's in a red lacy basque and I thought you might like to know that I'm wearing my favourite gold posy pouch. Come on lad, get your todger out."

"Already is old boy," Freddie said, pretending to be playing the game.

"Now just put my tease of a wife back on so she can finish what she started."

"She's already on her way back home...I think she's coming to give a hand you lucky lad."

There was more laughing in the background.

"Oh and Freddie darling, just one more thing that seems to have been forgotten in all this kerfuffle."

"What?"

"Happy Birthday my boy."

Seventeen

7.05 pm - Freddie was peering out of his front window.

He'd never known Uncle Roy to be late for anything, and certainly not for an opportunity to indulge in the lovely Lisa's excellent home cooking.

"Where on earth can he have got to?"

"Stop messing around with those drapes will you and come and light the candles."

Lisa was busy putting the finishing touches to the lavish dinner table she'd spent the last hour organising, fussing around it like it was laid for an extravagant royal banquet instead of the simple last minute get together that had been hurriedly arranged for Freddie's birthday.

"And stop fretting will you," she said. "He's barely five minutes late."

"Five minutes, for Roy that's only seconds away from a disaster."

Freddie peered into the night, shielding his eyes from the glare of the lights outside by cupping his hands to his forehead and leaning them against the cold window pane.

"Freddie!"

Before he was told off again he straightened the curtains and collected a lighter from the sideboard. Stepping towards the table he couldn't help but sneak a little squeeze of his wife's wonderfully delicate bum.

"Pervert," she squeaked cheerfully.

"Sorry, but there are certain things in life that this man could never resist. The table looks great by the way and I'm having a fantastic birthday, thanks."

He kissed her neck and she gave him a deliciously cheeky smile.

"I'm really sorry it all started so badly," she said softly. "I didn't mean to be such a..."

He gently spun her round to face him and kissed her, it was the only way he'd ever found to shut her up.

"It's okay, he said. "You've more than made up for it."

When she'd returned home all tearful and bleary eyed from the office, they'd had a good long chat, followed by a very pleasurable and productive cuddle.

After driving to the nearby town to drop off the sample pot at the 'Sexual Health and Wellbeing Clinic', Lisa had treated Freddie to a birthday lunch at one of the local pubs, happily allowing him to enjoy two pints of locally brewed ale.

They'd concluded a very pleasant afternoon together by wandering around the town, dodging the icy rain showers by taking shelter in several of the shops, and in each and every one of them the lovely

Lisa had found and bought Freddie a birthday gift.

She'd laughed all the time, even after Freddie got them both soaked again trying to get her back into Ann Summers for a third time.

It was just like old times.

"When you've lit those candles pop upstairs and make sure the radiators are turned up full in the bedrooms, both boys are staying over tonight."

She picked up the tea towel she'd been using to polish the glasses and headed back towards the kitchen, flicking it at his backside as she passed him.

"And hurry it up will you."

"We should charge those two for bed and breakfast," he called after her.

With the candles lit, he poured himself another glass of wine.

"They're just a couple of over indulged freeloaders," he shouted sarcastically in the general direction of the kitchen. "Why did you have to invite them to stay the night anyway? What kind of a sad fart spends his thirty seventh birthday getting drunk with two grumpy old men for company?"

He took a large guzzle.

Oscar appeared carrying a huge charger loaded with a glistening joint of beef surrounded by crispy roast potatoes and fluffy Yorkshire puddings.

Freddie pointed at him and yelled.

"Argh it's one of the grumpy old men."

"I see you've been at the bottle already Freddie darling? And I think someone should remind you my sweet boy that you're the very sad kind of thirty seven year old fart that can't be arsed to find himself some proper friends to get drunk with. Your uncle and I are only here to prevent you from boring your poor beleaguered wife to death. And less of your chutzpah about old men if you don't mind."

Oscar placed the food down on the table and playfully slapped Freddie's face.

"Roy and I are distinguished freeloaders, not just your everyday common old ones."

Freddie put his arm around his shoulders and gave him a quick peck on the cheek.

"Well if you promise not to be grouchy then you can stay," he smiled.

"And that by the way was a big thank you for your support earlier and nothing more."

Oscar looked quizzically over his glasses as his assailant took another gulp of wine.

"Lisa," he shouted, "Freddie's being unusually nice to me. Please advise."

"Ignore him and he'll go away," she said walking in with two more dishes of food.

She placed them down on the nearby sideboard.

Freddie looked puzzled.

"Why are you putting that lot over there? Normally everything goes on the table."

"Yes," Lisa yelled triumphantly.

"That's a fiver you owe me Oscar, I told you he wouldn't notice."

"Notice what?" Freddie exclaimed.

"There's no room for everything on the table Freddie because it's laid for five."

Freddie quickly scanned the table, there were five place settings, one more than he was expecting.

"And I bet Oscar you wouldn't notice."

"Why five, who else is coming?"

"It's a surprise Freddie, and if I'm not mistaken I can hear footsteps on the drive."

The doorbell rang.

"Quickly tell me," he begged. "Good surprise or bad?"

"Depends, but Oscar and I think good."

The doorbell rang impatiently.

"Go on and answer it then while we fetch in the rest of the food," Lisa laughed. "It'll only be Uncle Roy, not an ogre."

"Are you sure?" Oscar questioned. "Looking at all this food I would have put my money on an ogre turning up, or at the very least a mountain troll."

Freddie headed out into the hallway, but as he reached out to open the door he hesitated.

"Wait a minute," he said quietly to no one in particular. "Roy never rings the bell, he always knocks."

The bell rang again and made him jump.

"Come on Freddie, hurry up lad it's mightily cold out here."

The voice was unmistakably Roy's, his tone all bright and breezy.

Freddie opened the door and held out his hand ready to shake his uncle's, as was their custom.

"Hello Uncle Roy, glad you could make it."

"Happy Birthday lad."

Roy brushed his hand aside and enveloped him in the biggest bear hug ever.

Now Freddie was really confused.

Such an uncharacteristic open display of affection from Roy was a total mystery, and he was struggling to remember a time when this had ever happened before.

"Sorry we're a bit late only I've had a devil of a job parking the car."

"What?"

Before Freddie could say any more Roy released his vice-like grip.

"Of course you know Claire, don't you?" he said.

Claire emerged timidly from outside.

She held out a very expensive looking bottle of single malt.

"Hello Freddie, Happy Birthday."

She spoke softly and after handing him the bottle she gave him a big hug as well.

"Thank you for inviting me to your birthday dinner."

"Well don't just stand there gawping like a fish lad," Roy said, giving his nephew a hearty slap on the back. "Take the lady's coat and lead us to the food, we're starving. Here, let me help you with that."

He relieved his nephew of the bottle of whiskey and draped his heavy overcoat over Freddie's arm.

"The foods already on the table Uncle so go and sanitise your hands. Hurry up, get a wiggle on."

"Don't be daft lad, let's just eat."

Freddie almost dropped the coats.

"You carry on through Roy," Claire said. "I really must get out of these boots, they're crippling me."

"Just make sure you take care with my coat lad, it cost me more than your education." Roy instructed as he disappeared into the main room.

"Aha, so it is you after all Roy," Freddie called after him, but didn't get a reply.

Claire sat down on the chair in the hall and unzipped her boots.

"You don't mind me taking these off do you Freddie?"

"Not at all," he replied.

"Please make yourself at home. It's really nice to see you again."

"You too Freddie. This is a bit of a surprise for both of us eh?"

"The guys at THTC tried to tell me there was something going on but…Did he really say he'd had trouble parking a car?"

"Yes, we've had to park in the next street, there was nowhere in your road."

"And was he wearing stone washed jeans a sweater and no tie?"

"Yes, why?"

"Next you'll be telling me he's thrown away his briefcase and doesn't spend half his day with a packet of tissues and a bottle of hand gel."

"Well actually I've never seen him with either of those," she laughed.

"Seriously?"

"Sorry Freddie, but is there something wrong? You seem a little out of sorts."

"No no, it's all fine. It's just," he pointed towards the living room. "I never thought I would see the day when my overly obsessive, larger than life Uncle Roy would exchange his extraordinary bizarre habits for jeans, and a red v-necked sweater."

Claire was laughing again.

"Overly obsessive with bizarre habits? I can definitely say that you're not describing the man I came with tonight, at least I hope not."

"Then you couldn't have come with Royston 'I'll never own, drive or get into another car as long as I live' Hobbs. Oh it looks exactly like him but everything else, except the concern for his coat, is completely wrong."

"He's definitely himself from what I've seen, but don't worry too much about the car because he usually asks me to drive."

Roy's voice rang out clearly from the living room.

"Stop gossiping about me you two and get in here before everything goes cold. The meats carved and as usual Oscar's not waiting, he's already on his second Yorkshire pudding with a gallon of gravy."

"It is really is great to see you Claire."

Freddie held out a hand to help her up out of the chair.

"Please just ignore me and my doubting attitude, but I'm just not used to my uncle being this...well this completely normal. Whatever you're doing, please keep doing it."

He kissed her on the cheek as she rose.

"And that's the second time tonight I've had to do that and say thank you."

As they headed for the living room Freddie dumped the two coats in a crumpled heap over the handrail at the bottom of the stairs.

"But let's just see if there's any real change in his demeanour," he exclaimed.

"Sorry?" Claire asked.

"I'll explain it all later, in detail."

After being the perfect host and making sure everyone had a full glass of wine Freddie took his seat at the table between Oscar and Roy.

He was relaxed and enjoying the celebrations being given in his honour.

Claire's appearance with Roy had been a lovely surprise and now he was looking forward to amazing food, too much good wine and a whole heap of fun and laughter with this small group of folk he regarded as family.

"Well come on then, let's get started, tuck in."

"Birthday boy first," Freddie demanded.

"No chance," the two men either side of him said in unison. They all made a grab for the serving spoons and the charge for the food began.

There was no more chat during the next few minutes as they all concentrated hard on applying themselves fully to the task of transferring the deliciously aromatic fare from the dishes in the centre of the table and onto their plates.

To Claire it looked like a well rehearsed and choreographed table ballet as arms and spoons cavorted without a single spillage of the precious cargo.

Lisa could see that the newest guest to her well stocked table was completely mesmerised by the whole efficient routine and placed a reassuring hand on her arm.

"Please don't stand on ceremony Claire, it may look like there's plenty but these boys will make short work of it all."

"Better still," said Oscar, "Hold up your plate honey and these boys will show you how we give a girl a good time round here."

"Oh come on Oscar," Freddie snorted.

"You haven't shown any girl a good time since the discovery of all those pretty 'Glam Rock Boys' in the seventies."

"That's so true my boy...so true".

Claire held up her plate as requested and within seconds it was filled, everything neatly arranged.

Roy concluded the proceedings by offering her the gravy boat.

"One lump or two my dear?" he joked.

"Cheeky bugger."

Lisa threw a pea that hit him on the cheek.

"And how many lumps would you like on your face?"

Conversation started up again enthusiastically as they all set about the happy task of eating, praise being heaped on the chef.

"Incredible as usual Lisa...Delicious...You spoil us."

As the meal continued, Roy was keen to find out how preparations for Cinderella were going.

"It's all looking really good Uncle. We've spent two days putting the scenery together and I have to admit it's a really good set, lots of colour and easy to move."

"And what about all that very expensive lighting Sanjay insisted we have?"

"I went in for an hour while Lisa and Oscar were cooking. Steve and Scotty have spent all day rigging and by the time I left they'd got it all in place and programmed. We're well ahead of schedule and ready for the cast on Thursday as planned."

"I hope all this extra technology that keeps being added to my shows is going to be worth it. I really don't see the point."

"The whole thing will look fantastic I promise. A proper magical production."

"It always used to be about the show, now it's all about the special effects."

"Watch it Uncle, or you'll be turning into the next Stan Banks," Freddie joked. "And you know what we all think of him and his 'old' shows."

He picked up the wine bottle and topped up Roy's half empty glass.

"I suggest you have a few more of these and worry a little less about just how obscene your profits will be."

"Profit, I doubt it. Every year the costs go through the roof, I just don't understand why Sanjay..."

"Oh please, stop hogging the conversation you two old farts," Oscar interrupted. "Surely there must be something better to talk about than all this uninteresting theatrical drivel."

"Like what?"

"Well a blinding headache would be a good start. But Lisa and I would prefer to get to know this gorgeous young lady at our table a little better."

All eyes turned to Claire, she looked a little taken aback.

"Young, I wish. But okay, I suppose you need to know if you've invited a mad psychotic murderess into your home."

"Well if you are my dear girl you're in very good company," said Oscar.

For the next few minutes the attention intensified around the new girl at the table, questions being fired at her like a beleaguered contestant on Mastermind.

'Was she a local lass?'

'Hobbies and interests?'

'Where did she work?' and finally

'How did she get into theatre and had she enjoyed learning her role as the fairy in the pantomime?'

"To be honest, I'm finding it desperately hard to

remember all the lines," she said. "I don't think I've ever had so much to learn in such a short time."

"I bet our Roy's been overrun with lots of new things to learn as well." Oscar offered with a cheeky smile across the table.

"Like what," Roy asked with a frown, obviously not understanding the inference.

"Oh come on," Oscar continued with a grand flourish of his napkin. "Let's all be honest here and stop this polite wishy washy nonsense."

"Wishy Washy?" exclaimed Freddie. "I thought they were doing Cinderella this year not Aladdin."

"Not now Freddie." Oscar demanded.

"Sorry." Freddie stuffed a forkful of potato into his mouth while Oscar continued his grilling.

"What we're all desperate to know Claire is the sordid details of your past. Even better would be all the gossip about dear old Uncle Roy. Is he an absolute sex god, does he meet your needs?"

"Oh no, not at the dinner table please," Freddie spluttered.

"And why not lad? I have nothing to hide in that department," Roy insisted, puffing out his chest, a ridiculous smirk spreading across his face.

"Long term celibacy gives the older man an insatiable appetite for the love of a beautiful woman."

"Insatiable? Don't you men just love to dream," Lisa mocked.

"Sorry Claire, they're always a bit childish like this after a little alcohol. My advice is to just ignore them. Eventually they'll confuse each other, poor sods."

Claire seemed surprisingly at ease.

"No no, it's fine, I grew up with four brothers so I know exactly how this goes," she said giving Lisa a knowing smile.

"But I am going to have to disappoint you Oscar as my past is quite mundane, sorry."

"Aha, they all say that, just before skeletons are revealed."

"Oh believe me when I say I wish there were some, just so I had something interesting to impress you with."

"Okay then, tell us on a scale of one to ten how boring is Roy compared with your boring past?"

"Oscar, can we please stop talking about my boring uncle."

"I wasn't, I was enquiring about your uncle's boring."

"Can we not mention my Uncle Roy and boring in the same sentence again, please."

"Nothing wrong with boring lad, in fact I'm sure we can all be boring at times."

"I haven't been boring since 1997," Oscar sighed.

"Now I have images of both of them boring in my head, what a shitty birthday I'm having."

"I don't know about you Claire but I'm getting bored," said Lisa.

"What right at this very moment? You lucky girl," Claire replied.

Both girls started giggling while the boys looked on bemused.

"I hope you ladies are not suggesting that we were using 'Boring' as some sort of euphemism for sex?" Oscar demanded.

"Can we just get back to pantomime for a minute please," said Freddie.

"Why."

"Because I want to change the subject...and before we were so rudely interrupted by Nosey Norma here," Freddie poked Oscar's arm with his finger and gave it a twist. "I was about to tell you some good news Roy."

"What news?" Roy asked eagerly. "Did Brian tell you the sales figures?"

"Yep."

Freddie took a gulp of his wine to eke out the suspense.

"And?"

"As of close of business tonight, Cinderella sales are already near the ninety percent mark, and the trustees are asking if you want to take the option of a further week."

"Yes please. That's so much better than I was expecting and thanks to Claire here I think we're going to put on our best production ever."

"Well thank you for making me your fairy."

"That news deserves a toast," Freddie cheered.

"To Magical Productions and Claire the Fairy."

"Magical Productions and Claire the Fairy."

They raised and chinked glasses offering their heartiest congratulations.

"I have some good news to announce as well," Lisa piped up above the cheering.

"IGL has been nominated for an award for its continuing contribution to the fashion industry."

The excited cheering began again.

"And there's more," she continued.

"Oscar, my dear partner and our good friend here, has been recognised as well, for giving over forty years of iconic service to the industry."

"That news deserves a toast," Freddie cheered.

"To IGL and Oscar the Fairy."

"IGL and Oscar the...Freddie!"

After another round of chinking glasses they all stood up and went around hugging each other, enthusiastically patting backs.

Freddie once again felt his confusion returning at his uncle's open show of affection towards everyone. As Roy grabbed him and gave him a massive squeeze he could contain himself no longer.

"Can you please tell me what you've done with the real Uncle Roy," Freddie called over to Claire as they all sat back down again.

"Aren't I allowed to be a little bit more casual occasionally lad?"

"I'm hoping we're a bit more than occasional or casual," Claire said, giving Roy a big grin.

"Well personally I think it's great you've found someone you can be happy with Roy," Lisa offered, cocking a playful sneer at her husband.

"And I do too my dear," Freddie sneered back.

"And I'm not being critical of the new Roy, I just can't believe how completely different he is."

"Well Freddie my sweet and wonderful hubbie, I just think you don't want to admit that you hate change as much as your uncle used to. I for one love the new Roy."

"Thank you my dear," said Roy.

"Oh come on, surely you just can't ditch the real Roy?" Freddie teased. "You know, the man who always wore a suit and constantly worries about germs and crashing cars, and enjoys telling me how I've wasted a great talent and I'm too old for kids. As for all these hugs, you've never allowed people to touch you."

"Maybe I didn't, but that kind of behaviour is probably the cause of my loneliness. Thanks to this beautiful lady I can see the person I was isn't the person I want to be, and for once in my life I am actually having fun doing the things I haven't done for years."

"I bet you are," Oscar said with a wink at Claire.

"I'm sorry, I didn't realise you felt lonely Uncle. I wish I'd done more now."

"You and the lovely Lisa did plenty. I was always well looked after and everything else was down to me, not you. But from now on I'm going to be different."

"Then I'll need to get used to hugging my new Uncle Roy."

"Come on you soppy pair," Lisa exclaimed.

"It's just the 'I love you' phase brought on by the alcohol my dear," Oscar joked. "It'll soon pass and then they'll get all serious and depressing."

"Oh please," said Lisa. "No more tears today."

"Drink quickly then and we can bypass serious and depressing and go straight for comatose."

"Oh and there's something else you need to know Freddie," Roy said, his tone quite matter of fact. "And now is probably as good a time as any to tell you."

"You mean while you two are still bestest buddies," Oscar asked.

"More because he's slightly drunk and in a forgiving mood I hope."

"Please don't tell me there's some kind of major production change with less than a week to go."

"It's nothing like that lad, but I'm aware that

there is something in the show that might upset you...personally, so you have to know."

Freddie's fork, piled with peas, stopped half way between the plate and his mouth.

"What could be personal to me about a pantomime," he asked.

"Well there's a question and a half," said Oscar.

Roy continued after the others had finished laughing.

"Well, you know it's traditional for us to include a song from our next production as a preview?" He paused for an acknowledgement.

"Well yes," Freddie said.

Half the peas fell off his fork and into his lap.

"Spit it out Roy the tension is causing Freddie's peas to throw themselves into the afterlife," Oscar joked.

"Next year's production is going to be 'Backstage' and the song they're performing in the pantomime is your song...sorry lad."

Lisa looked across at Freddie expecting to see his highly spirited mood disappear.

"Well that's a bit of a shock," she said in his direction. "Are you all right Freddie?"

Freddie just popped the peas into his mouth.

"Is that all?" he said spluttering half of them back out again. "I thought we were going to have some kind of insurmountable issue the way you were acting."

"Are you saying you're okay with that?"

"Why wouldn't I be?"

"I'm sorry but I don't get it," Claire butted in. "Backstage is one of the best underrated shows ever, and that song, The Other Side of Me is sensational.

Why wouldn't Freddie be okay with it?"

Lisa started "It's because…"

But Freddie interrupted her.

"A very good and timely question Claire, and one I think deserves to be properly answered. Roy and my lovely wife here believe that I'm haunted by my past because I had a great opportunity once. But it's time they knew that my demons have long gone, and for good."

He took another sip of wine and gestured for Oscar to fill him up again.

"You see Claire, back in '98 I was supposed to be in the UK tour of Backstage, I was cast to play the part of Cory, the principal who sings that song."

"I never knew you were an actor. In all the years I've been coming to THTC no one's ever said anything."

"That's because he's never told anyone."

"That's because no one outside of this family ever needed to know."

"That's such a great role, what happened?"

"Someone shouted 'Break a leg' so I did."

"I'm really sorry I shouldn't have asked."

"No Claire I'm glad you did because I...we really shouldn't mind talking about this. Except that my family here don't like to mention it for fear it might upset me. They believe that particular twist of fate ruined my life, and at the time I probably thought so too."

"You were devastated."

"Yes I was. But now, sixteen years later, you guys still think that losing that dream ultimately ruined my life, even though I don't feel the same way."

"You've never said anything like that before."

"Probably because I feel guilty about admitting it. Especially in front of my agent, who incidentally lost a lot of money on this project."

"It wasn't about the money lad."

"I know Uncle. But that never stopped me from feeling bad about it."

"You had such a talent. Nobody thought the injury was as bad as it was."

"Do you remember dad used to say that everything in life happens for a reason, good or bad there's always a purpose?"

"One of his favourite's that one."

"And he genuinely believed what he said, and although it took me a long time to accept it, I think he was absolutely right. That injury took me off the stage I loved, but it gave me the life I have now, which I think is just perfect. It's a life I might not have had but for that fateful day. So you see, everything for a reason."

"Like a 'Sliding Doors' moment," said Claire. "I cried all the way through that movie."

"Absolutely, so did I."

"But you loved performing, you lived to sing," Lisa insisted.

"You're right, I did then, and I admit there's been many times since when I've wondered what I might be doing now. But 'what if's' don't matter to me anymore because I wouldn't swap what I have for anything."

With that he started shovelling up more peas again.

Oscar was staring over his glasses at Freddie who was now merrily loading more food onto his plate.

"You're a bigger drama queen than me you daft

bugger."

He wiped his eyes with his serviette.

"But I have to admit he says the nicest things. Ooh I could just squish him."

"Well it would appear that the alcohol has dropped us all off at the 'serious' plaza," Lisa said to Claire. "So hold very tight please everyone this could get bumpy."

"I've just had a great idea," said Roy.

"How about I offer Freddie the part of Cory in next year's production?"

"Thanks, but I've got a job already, I'll be stage managing the show."

"You've just admitted to thinking about what might have been, so I'm giving you the chance to find out and keep the life you love. Maybe like me you should consider what might have been."

"Please don't waste time thinking what might have been Uncle. You'll only discover that if you did waste time in the past there's nothing you can do about it in the present, except waste more time thinking about it. "

Oscar held up a hand.

"Can we go back to a boring conversation please. This is way over my head."

"Then it's time for another toast," Freddie announced loudly.

"What to this time?"

"It's your birthday lad, make a wish and we'll toast it," Roy said.

"Well there's nothing I can think of at the..."

"Let's toast your sperm Freddie," Lisa blurted out.

"I'm sorry, for a moment then I thought you

wanted to toast my sperm."

"We dropped a sample off at the clinic today so I'm wishing for a good healthy sperm count to make babies."

Oscar cringed.

"Well okay, the toast is Freddie's sperm."

"Can we all stop talking about my sperm please as they're starting to develop a complex, not to mention poor Claire here is wondering what kind of family discusses this sort of thing at the dinner table."

"Oh this is great. I haven't had this much fun since Oldklahoma."

"Then the toast has been made," Oscar insisted.

"Just a minute though," Freddie held up a hand and turned to Roy who was looking concerned.

"You okay Uncle."

"I'm just feeling sorry for you my lad."

"Well don't, we're going to be fine whatever happens, and I appreciate you're kindness in the past."

Roy looked puzzled.

"I know you were trying to ease the blow when I found out the truth about the family secret."

"How did I do that?"

"When you kept telling me in the Lotus I was too old to have kids."

Uncle and nephew were starting to slur their words.

"That was very thoughtful of you."

"Not really lad," Roy laughed.

"I meant every single word of it."

Eighteen

Friday 20th 8.12 am - Freddie was enjoying a coffee in the green room with Sanjay, the pantomime's director.

Yesterday's technical rehearsal had gone really well and they'd managed to run through every scene except for the finale of act one. Sanjay had been keen to leave this part of the show alone until he'd had the chance to work out with Freddie how it should run. He considered it to be the pivotal moment of the whole show and the staging of it had to be just right.

"This scene has to be perfect Freddie. It may seem very complex but it isn't really, it just has to progress precisely with the timing of the music. There's a great dance routine and the perfect song and it all ends with the magical appearance of the crystal coach to whisk Cinders off to the ball."

"Would you prefer silent tears or uncontrollable sobbing?"

"Both if possible please."

They had a great rapport and really enjoyed

working together.

Sanjay's main ambition was driven by a genuine passion to create a world of make believe for every member of an audience to meander through. Freddie appreciated the chance this gave him to put structure to a dream, adding his own unique touches of magic.

Their partnership had delivered some spectacular shows over the years, which had often received a very strong emotional response from the spectators, and the critics.

"I want the set to feel dark and dingy as it opens, I need to sense the Prince's despair that he may never see Cinders again, and even if he does will she fall madly in love with him?. Think night time in the woods, or even better a graveyard, all misty and spooky. Can we get a hooting owl?"

"Single hoot or a whole cacophony?" Freddie was taking notes.

"I just need it to set the scene Freddie. I'm fairly sure the last thing this show needs is any more hams pushing for a bigger part."

"So you don't need the tap dancing owl this time then?"

"Honestly man, your imagination is so much weirder than mine. Have we got a tap dancing owl?"

"No."

"Then I'll have to settle for a non dancing single hooter."

"I'll get Scotty to sort one out and stick it on the show disc."

"Well that conjures up a whole new image, but moving on. As Cinders enters still in her rags the lighting state still needs to be quite dark, but I want to see some colours like reds and violets."

Freddie interrupted, "Sorry matey, but I reckon the best thing is to get out front and plot the lighting as we go. What time are the cast in?"

"I've only got those involved with this scene coming in initially, but breakfast is at nine forty five followed by warm-ups. I want them to be on stage for ten thirty if possible."

"Then we'll save some time if we don't go through this twice. Take your coffee and sit out in the auditorium with a comms pack and I'll switch everything on and go up to the cave. Tell me what you want I'll set it."

"But don't we need the scenery in position?"

"It's all set ready. The crystal coach is on a motor pull so I can do everything from the box. All you have to do is imagine the actors."

"You're so organised you should be running the world instead of just this theatre."

"Trust me Sanjay, this is all the world I want."

"A wasted talent if you ask me and definitely the world's loss."

"You've been working with my uncle for too long mate, you're even starting to sound like him.

10.15 am - In under two hours Freddie had finished plotting the lighting.

He'd even programmed the smoke machines to give the desired effect without swamping the stage with a pea-soup fog.

"It's looking great Freddie, just how I imagined it in my head, thanks."

"As always the pleasure is all yours Sanjay. Coffee? There may even be some breakfast left if we're quick."

"Not for me thanks, I need to make sure everyone's here and ready," he handed back his comms pack.

"Sorry, I almost forgot." Sanjay looked very apologetic. "We'll need an offstage microphone for this scene as well."

"Okay, where will you need it positioned?"

"Not sure, but I should imagine Alson will need to be able to see the MD."

"Alson? Alson Var?"

"Oh shit," Sanjay exclaimed.

"I was hoping to give you a heads up, but it seems you know him already."

"Never met the guy, but I have heard the stories."

Alson Var had been a much talked about thorn in Roy's side for years, the topic of many a conversation at the 'Lotus Leaf'.

Without doubt he had a great singing voice, but over the years Roy had received more grief from this one performer than all the others combined.

He was always demanding more money, better accommodation and had often insisted he deserved the lifestyle enjoyed by Superstars rather than the reasonably good performer that he was.

"Nobody has mentioned his name at any of the production meetings. What's going on?"

"Sorry Freddie, it was a last minute change we had to make. The guy we had lined up has let us down."

"Well from what I've heard he's the last person I'd expect in find in a pantomime."

"We didn't get a choice, and now I've had the pleasure I know exactly why Mr Var is the only decent vocalist available at such short notice."

"But why do you need him. AJ, the Prince has a great voice?"

"It's my fault Freddie. I wanted a tableau, like a dream scene, with the song being sung offstage."

"So Roy found you Alson."

"Unfortunately yes. But you're right, and luckily for us, he doesn't want to be seen dead in a panto, so he turns up, sings the song and then buggers off. You'll only have to put up with his antics for a few minutes each night, and he does have an incredible voice."

"To go with his incredibly bad attitude so I'm led to believe. Okay Sanjay, I'll get it sorted. We'll set up a booth for him, with monitors so he can see and hear Geoff."

"It's a nice song Freddie," Sanjay said as they headed for the green room. "It's from the musical Backstage. I'm sure you'll get to like it, even if you don't get to like Mr Var."

"I already do...and I know I won't."

Almost as soon as Freddie had completed setting up the sound booth Sanjay was back, trailing behind a tall well dressed man.

"Alson this is Freddie, the stage manager."

Freddie knew Alson wouldn't even acknowledge his existence so didn't bother to hold out a hand. But he offered a cursory greeting, then winked a Sanjay.

"Anything you need Alson, please just ask," he added.

"Well for a start you and the rest of your fucking motley crew will call me Mr Var. Do that and we'll get on just fine.

"We all work as a team back here Alson,

everyone is an integral part of this show."

"Don't try being fucking smart with me pops, or you may find yourself looking for another job. Don't confuse yourself into thinking you're anything fucking special."

"I'm employed by the theatre and not Magical Productions so if you think…"

"Freddie please," Sanjay interrupted.

"Oh it's okay director, let the chief scenery shifter have his say, but I guarantee you pops that your poor old Uncle Roy won't be very happy if you piss me off."

"Then please accept my sincerest apologies and welcome to my stage sir," Freddie said sarcastically.

"But I insist…"

"Freddie please." Sanjay looked panicked.

"But I insist," Freddie repeated, "That you curb your language when you're on the stage…please."

Alson brushed the comment aside with a wave of his hand.

"I need fresh iced water available at all times and an antiseptic spray for my throat. Make sure both are in the booth every night."

"I'll sort that out," Sanjay quickly offered before Freddie exploded.

"And just you make sure that none of your monkeys get in my way pops, okay?"

"How about I keep them on the other side of the stage, just in case you catch fleas off them?"

"How very fucking original, I bet you've been saving that one for ages."

He turned to Sanjay, "I've had enough of this director, I've been shown where to stand so now I'm off home."

"But we're going to rehearse the scene shortly, we need you to sing the song."

"My contract starts at the dress, so I'll be back here for that this afternoon, and not before."

He spun round and headed off. "Oh and pops," he called back. "Make sure I get a new microphone, I don't want one that stinks like shit."

"With pleasure chap," Freddie shouted after him.

"And if you call me pops once more I'll..."

Alson Var was gone.

Freddie turned to Sanjay and smiled.

"I like him already."

"Keep the peace Freddie, please."

"You know me my friend, laid back and comatose are the only two states I possess."

"Roy tells me he knows exactly how to get what he wants."

"Then let's hope," he said patting his friend gently on the shoulder. "He's as good a singer as he is an idiot, because he's exceptionally good at being an idiot."

Nineteen

Monday 23rd 7.00 pm - There was a palpable air of expectancy coursing through the theatre.

The technical rehearsals had been two days of almost problem free preparation for the cast and had culminated in one of the slickest 'dress' performances Freddie could ever remember.

Amid intense excitement Magical Productions pantomime Cinderella had then 'unofficially opened' at the weekend, with a matinee on both days for audiences exclusively 'by invitation only'. These were mainly the family and friends of the cast and regular patrons of THTC.

Everything had gone well and Freddie even had to admit to Sanjay that the legendary Mr Var did indeed have a very good voice.

"It's just a shame he doesn't sing with any feeling," he'd added.

"Probably because he doesn't have any, and certainly not for anybody other than himself."

Tonight was the official opening of the show and a very special occasion.

The foyer was crammed with influential folk from the world of performing arts, as well as the ladies and gentlemen of the press, local council dignitaries, and the advertisers and sponsors of the production.

Volunteers, sporting trays of complementary alcoholic beverages and delicious titbits of finger food, moved among the guests, and members of the cast worked the crowd with their natural charm.

With everything set and ready backstage Freddie was making his way through the crush in the foyer to find Lisa and Oscar, who appeared to be deep in conversation with Her Ladyship the Mayor.

"That's not good," Freddie muttered to himself.

He quickened his pace towards his target, stopping briefly to whisper in Claire's ear.

When this current Mayor had taken up her post she'd quickly discovered that the offices of a prestigious and very popular lifestyle magazine were based in her own town and considered this would give her the perfect opportunity for a bit of self promotion.

On an almost daily basis Lisa had been bombarded with demands from the Mayor's personal assistant to publish a feature article about her illustrious career. The correspondent had continually stated that 'As 'Her Ladyship' was the epitome of elegance and good taste' she would be the perfect role model for the modern career woman.

The official response from the desk of the editor

was that they didn't get involved in politics.

At a recent meeting of local businesses the Mayor had remarked to Oscar that her inclusion in the magazine would dramatically increase readership. He'd replied that IGL was only interested in promoting all that was new, beautiful and fashionable in the world and she didn't fit into any of those categories, or more recently her clothes.

"It's hard to believe that a publication like yours would have any interest in sponsoring an insignificant event like this," Freddie heard her say.

He saw Lisa nudge Oscar into silence.

"It's a family affair Madam Mayor."

"But what has a play got to do with fashion? I really don't understand."

"Fashion and theatre are all part of art and culture, they go together perfectly. Even so, as a local business we're keen to encourage local talent," Lisa said.

"Someone has to support the people of Swelford," Oscar added with a sneer.

The Mayor frowned and raised a finger.

"What are you suggesting?"

"Excuse me Madam Mayor," Freddie interrupted.

"But the guys from the Gazette are keen to get a picture of you with some of the cast on the stage."

Claire was right behind him.

"Madam Mayor, may I introduce you to Claire, she'll take you where you need to go, and thank you for the taking time to come and see our show."

"And who are you in this play?" the Mayor bumbled at Claire.

Oscar was hoping that Claire would have the balls to smack her in the face with her wand and tell her to take a wild guess, but she didn't.

"I'm Cinderella's Fairy Godmother," she said politely, then added with a laugh as she led her away, "Either that or I've stolen her sparkly wings and enormous fairy-godmother-like wand."

Freddie kissed Lisa on the cheek.

"How's everything going gorgeous?"

"Really well I think," Lisa gave his arm a squeeze. "I always get excited when panto comes to town."

"I don't," Oscar grumped. "But I do find it amazing how much more people indulge themselves when everything is free."

"Just because you're paying the bill tonight. But I know the feeling, it happens like that all the time round at my house."

"I get nothing for free from you my boy, I pay with my sanity."

"And you're well overdrawn at that bank."

Lisa laughed.

"Anyway, how do you both fancy coming backstage later on? It's not a busy show this year so I've given Scotty the chance to run the book."

"What are we betting on then?" Oscar asked, "And who's the favourite?"

"It's not that kind of book, silly," said Lisa.

"In the theatre Oscar 'the book' is a complete show script and music score which contains all the technical cues. The person who 'runs the book' controls the entire show, calling the cues to tell everyone involved exactly what to do and precisely when to do it."

"Isn't that supposed to be your job?"

"It's the job I usually do yes, but theoretically it's

the deputy stage manager that 'runs the book' leaving the SM free to sort out any problems. As we're only a small theatre we don't have the personnel to run it like that. But I try to give the others a chance at taking charge whenever possible so if I can't be here, well you can guess the rest."

Oscar wasn't listening.

"That lady over there has just put a bottle in her bag," he exclaimed. "That's just rude, I'll be back in a tick."

"And I better go and make sure he doesn't start a fight. We'll come and see you later sweetie."

Lisa chased after her partner.

"Freddie." One of the volunteers tapped him on the shoulder.

"I think you're wanted," she said, pointing towards the office where Brian was frantically gesturing in his general direction.

"I'm so popular tonight," he said, taking a couple of tuna rolls off her tray.

"Thanks."

He ambled across the foyer. "What the panic Brian?"

"Roy's in the office Freddie, he seems rather upset about something."

"Oh dear, that's not like him at all. Let's hope he's not having fairy problems, rubbing up against all those sequins can give you a nasty rash."

As soon as he stepped into the office Roy started.

"You know me Freddie, I've always looked after my acts. For years I've booked good work for that ungrateful man and he repays me by upsetting nearly every customer I've ever had. Now I'm the customer and it's my turn to be on the receiving end of his absurdly stupid ideas."

"Problems with Var?"

"He's demanding more money."

Roy looked devastated.

"Humour him until after Christmas then just replace him, find someone else."

"There isn't anyone else available, and even if there was I can't terminate his contract without it costing me a pile of money, and he knows it."

"Seriously?"

"He's particularly pissed with you Freddie. As well as the money he demands you stop harassing him about his 'occasional stress induced profanities' as he calls it."

"No, that's not going to happen. When he's on my stage he will follow my rules."

"Please Freddie. It's press night and I have far too much to lose. Just turn a blind eye this once."

"I have standards Roy you know that. We should never compromise on the principle that respect and courtesy are important in this business."

His voice trailed off. Roy could see his mind had wandered off somewhere.

"Does he have a Magical Productions contract?" Freddie suddenly asked.

"What?"

"I want to know which contract he's working under."

"I don't see why, but if you must know I didn't see the point of changing his original Hobbs Enterprise contract so I just extended it until the end of January."

"Brilliant."

"Freddie please don't do anything rash."

"It's okay Uncle, you know I would never disrupt a show or damage your reputation, but respect and courtesy are the only things we have left. If Mr Var continues his antics he needs to be reminded of that."

"Please Freddie don't aggravate him.""

"You have a great show so stop worrying. Now, on a different matter, Lisa and Oscar are coming backstage for a drink once the shows up and running so why not join us?"

"I didn't think you allowed alcohol backstage."

"I don't, but if you conceal it in a bottle of fruit juice or cola then I won't notice, will I?"

8.20 pm - Fifty minutes into the first act and the pantomime was in full swing and going well if the audience reaction was anything to go by.

The Hobbs family, Oscar and Sanjay were gathered around the props table at the rear of the stage in the wings. Having smuggled in some party food and drink they were indulging in a small premature celebration of the show's success whist the cast and crew bustled around them.

"How's he doing?" Roy asked pointing at Scotty, who was huddled at the control desk with his head buried deep in a mass of paper.

"He's a natural, he hasn't missed a single beat of the music."

"Does this mean there will be some nights off for you?" Lisa asked hopefully.

"No promises, but probable. We'll see."

"I still think it's unnatural to spend so much time in the dark," said Oscar, "It's making me feel like a vampire."

"In tight leather trousers with his shirt off?"

"You know me so well Roy."

"Well I just love it," Sanjay exclaimed. "You can hide from reality in the dark."

"The more often I meet you Sanjay the more I'm convinced you're a long lost relative of the Hobbs family," said Lisa. "That was straight out of the book of Freddie sayings."

Sanjay put on a sad face "I wish I had a family," he said.

"He's a snotty nosed ragamuffin orphan just like me," Freddie said.

"The proper one sock up and one down variety?" Lisa asked.

"I'm truly authentic with dirty knees and a dead frog as a friend."

"Then I'll adopt you immediately and you're invited to the Hobbs family Christmas lunch, and I won't take no for an answer."

"Seriously, thanks."

"Twelve o'clock on the dot, but please don't bring the frog."

They all toasted 'Sanjay Hobbs' and the lads slapped his back heartily.

"Get ready," Oscar said. "Someone's coming."

Every time the stage door had opened they'd turned to merrily welcome whoever it was to the stage with a toast.

This time the party atmosphere fell off the cliff as Alson Var strutted over to the group.

Freddie looked at his watch.

"You're a bit early Mr Var," he said politely.

"There's still some time before you're needed. Have you been called?"

"No, but I was looking for the producer here."

He turned to face Roy. "And it appears I found him just in time. I want an answer to my earlier question."

"You mean your demand for more money," said Freddie.

"This is a private matter pops, just mind your own fucking business."

"What," Lisa growled.

Freddie quickly held up his hand and shook his head towards her.

"There's a show going on sweetie, can we keep this quiet please."

He wasn't really that concerned about any noise as he knew the heavy drapes would baffle all but the loudest of screams, but he wanted the others to let him handle this his way.

They all got the message.

"Actually Mr Var everything that happens in this theatre is my business, especially when it concerns my family."

"Oh whatever," Var scoffed. "I just want to make sure that Uncle Roy here understands that I must have an answer to my earlier request before I sing tonight."

"That's an interesting turn of phrase Mr Var, are you using 'before' to mean 'ahead of' or as 'an incentive to'?"

"Ahead of or as an incentive to," Var mimicked in a squeaky voice. "Oh don't we think we're fucking clever pops."

"Watch your language Mr Var, there are ladies present."

"Do you think I give a shit? Look I have something this show needs and I want a better price for it. Supply and demand it's that simple."

"He's right Freddie."

"No he's not Roy. This type of behaviour is completely unacceptable."

"It's called looking after number one, and as I see it there's not a fucking thing you can do about it."

"Temper your language Mr Var or leave my stage."

"You really believe you can do that, don't you?"

He shook his head.

"Well guess what, I'm going to call your bluff old man, I'm not going to be fucking told what I can say by a jumped up stage hand, and I'll not be singing either until you apologise for being a prick."

"I have nothing to apologise for, you on the other hand have a contract."

"You will apologise and Uncle Roy here will write me a brand new contract offering me a better deal or the shit hits the fan."

"I will go to any lengths to protect my family and its reputation Mr Var, and I mean anything."

Freddie looked directly at his family and smiled. Roy could tell that he had a plan.

Lisa instantly knew what the plan was and had to bite her lip, hard.

"Oh how fucking sentimental."

"You will temper your language and you will sing the song as per your contract."

"Make me."

"Do you remember the details of your contract Mr Var?"

Freddie reached down to the table and picked up a folder.

"Oh great, it's time to review my fucking

contract. Read me the bit where a grand a week has just been added to my remuneration pops."

"Mind your language please Mr Var," Freddie said politely.

He opened the folder, took out some papers and started to read.

"The client will fulfil his obligation as agreed with the customer and will not withdraw his services at any time without prior warning and due reason."

"I see what you're trying to do here pops, but we both know that I will sing the fucking song and there will be no breach of contract because you and your uncle will comply with my request, there's no other choice."

Freddie continued to read.

"The client through his actions guarantees not to bring the agency into disrepute and promises to represent the same in a courteous and respectful manner at all times."

"Blah de fucking blah. Stop pissing about and realise this. I don't care what you think is right or wrong, and the quicker you realise that the better. You will apologise, Roy will write a cheque and I will sing the fucking stupid song, but you're running out of time."

One of the volunteer crew had come over to the group with a message from Scotty.

"Three minutes to places please Mr Var."

"See, what did I fucking tell you?"

"This will be my last warning Mr Var, please mind your language."

"Or what?"

Freddie ignored him and continued to read.

"Once signed the client fully accepts the terms

and conditions of this contract without exclusion and will not, under any circumstance, attempt to renegotiate any part of the agreed contract directly or indirectly with the customer without the express permission of the agent."

"This is all very interesting, but the clock is still ticking."

"Well as I see it Mr Var you can't get what you want without breaking the terms of your contract. It's all a bit like the Merchant of Venice and his pound of flesh," Freddie said cheerfully. "What do you think Roy?"

"Oh really?" Var laughed and turned to the producer.

"So what do you think Roy? You're about a gnat's bollock away from being ruined and your idiot nephew is quoting Shakespeare. I suggest you step in and stop all this nonsense before it's too late."

"It's starting to sound like you're losing control Mr Var. This isn't quite going to plan and things are getting desperate for you."

"What?"

"Last chance Alson, step up to the microphone or you're in breach of contract."

The volunteer was back looking panicked.

"Scotty says you have about two minutes before the scene change, places please."

"Please tell the DSM we'll be there in time," Freddie said calmly.

Sanjay had finally had enough.

"Freddie you must..."

Roy grabbed his arm and put a finger to his lips.

"It's all going to be okay," he said.

"You reckon Roy, I think you're totally fucked."

"Far from it," he replied. "I reckon we're about to witness something very special."

"Then you better pray for a fucking miracle."

"That's it, get him and his foul mouth off my stage, call security if necessary."

"Oh this should be fun, I want to stick around and watch this fiasco."

"Then buy a ticket like everyone else. If you're still in my theatre at the interval you'll get to see how pissed I am at being called pops. Goodbye sonny boy."

He grabbed Lisa's hand and quickly headed toward Scotty and the booth.

"What the?" Var protested.

"Looks like someone doesn't like the way you've been singing his song.

"His song?"

"May I suggest that if you call someone's bluff you should at least make sure you know what you're up against. A lesson for the future I feel, not that you have one with me. You're in breach of contract and you're fired Mr Var."

Oscar and Sanjay stood by Roy with the intention of 'guiding' his ex-client from the stage, but faced with such overwhelming odds even Var didn't fancy his chances, especially against the scary looking gay guy, so he raced off on his own.

Roy turned to Sanjay.

"Most of the staff witnessed that, so get around to the other side of the stage and make sure they know everything is okay."

"How can I tell them everything okay when I've no idea what's happening."

"Just trust me, now hurry."

Freddie tapped Scotty's shoulder.

"All right lad?" he said, giving him a reassuring smile.

"What's going on Boss? Steve's just said he's seen Mr Var leave the stage."

"He's decided not to join in the party tonight. How long till the change?"

Scotty looked at his stopwatch.

"Just over a minute. Everyone's in place but the cast waiting on stage right are worried that something's gone wrong."

"It's being sorted."

"And now I'm starting to panic Boss, what about Mr Var?"

"Listen lad, nothing's changed for you so just carry on with the great job you've been doing so far, I'll sort the rest."

Freddie's mind was racing.

"You okay sweetie?" Lisa asked.

He nodded and realised he was still gripping her hand, probably a little too tightly judging by the look on her face, he let go and gave her a smile.

"This seemed like a good idea a few minutes ago. I just need to relax a bit."

Reaching over he grabbed the spare comms pack, knowing something familiar would distract him. As he put the headset on his ears were filled with loud anxious chatter, everyone was talking at once, exactly what was needed to calm his mind.

"SM on comms."

Freddie announced, quickly turning the volume down to his earpiece.

Everyone but Steve stopped talking.

"What's going on Boss?"

"I'll explain later but for now everyone please listen up. You may have guessed we have an issue down here but it's sorted. From now on I only want to hear the DSM and standbys on comms please, nothing else. Call it Scotty, by the book lad."

"Standby end of 6 in 40, Lx cue 159 black out. Strike set stage right. Sound only follow through cue 160/57. Cue 161 fly 4 in 162 fly 22 in. All standby 20."

"Lx waiting."

"Stage ready."

"Sound ready."

"Fly 4 and 22 standing by."

The scene was coming to an end and in the apparent chaos of the change there was structure and order. For Freddie it was a moment of reality and what he was about to do was just pure fantasy.

He felt his composure returning and his pulse slowing as the unnoticed backstage drill continued at pace.

"Lx cue 159 blackout, Sound follow through cue 160/57 go." Scotty called.

All the lights went out as the audience applauded and the cast on stage raced off. A crescendo of music started to create the atmosphere for the coming scene.

"Strike set, cue 161 fly 4 in go. Standby on 22." Scenery and backdrops were moving into position at the youngsters command.

"Lx waiting."

"4 in, standing by on 22."

Freddie stood and watched over the DSM's shoulder, he knew he had a little time yet and hoped it would be enough.

"Cue 162 fly 22 go. Standby Lx cue 163 sound cue

163/58, cue 166 fly 4 out."

Hidden haze machines were filling the stage with wisps of fine white mist.

"22 in, standing by on 4."

"Lx waiting"

"Sound waiting."

'This never ceases to thrill me' Freddie thought.

"Stage right clear, set and ready."

"Lx cue 163 sound cue 163/58 go" Scotty called.

Dark blue lights lit up a misty stage, dimly revealing a night sky with twinkling stars cutting brightly through the haze. The music settled into a light mystical orchestration of strings and woodwind.

"Standby sound cue 164/59, Lx cue 165."

"Standing by."

"How long is the music lead for the song lad?" Freddie asked.

Scotty consulted his stopwatch.

"The mic goes live in ninety Boss," he said.

"Sound cue 164/59 go, fly 4 go."

Somewhere out on stage an owl gave a single hoot. As the lights brightened the front gauze lifted causing a movement of the air which made the mist spiral upwards.

Cinderella entered from the opposite side still dressed in her servant clothes, excitedly clutching her invitation to the ball. A follow spot picked her up as she started to dance happily through the mist.

"That's it Boss, 30 seconds. Somebody needs to be in that booth."

AJ the Prince stood nearby looking quizzically in their direction, a slight tinge of concern showed on his face.

Freddie took a deep breath.

"SM off comms," he said and removed his headset and placed it back on the desk.

"I still can't believe you're actually going to do this," Lisa said as they moved away from the control desk and stood looking into the booth.

Freddie could clearly see the friendly face of Geoff the MD on the monitor in front of the microphone.

"Strangely enough, neither can I," he said kissing her on the cheek. "If you won't be too embarrassed to stay with me, I could really use a Lisa-full of inspiration right now."

"I'm so proud of you, of course I will."

Scotty turned round and gave a 'thumbs up' and as the Prince entered stage left Freddie stepped into the booth and gently sighed.

The music changed and sixteen years vanished with the first bar.

He closed his eyes for a second and heard Lisa catch her breath softly beside him. Then he looked at the monitor and waited for his cue, wondered if his long time friend would know.

As the beauty of a perfectly choreographed romance unfolded on his stage Freddie sang.

"Dreams hide in the shadows,
Yet unspoken through fear,
And I dare not reveal them
Just in case she won't hear."

Looking down at the monitor for his next cue it was obvious that Geoff knew exactly who was singing. Freddie continued.

*"So afraid of rejection,
And the pain of before,
Here concealed in the darkness
Will love pass by my door?"*

He glanced across the stage at Cinderella and the Prince dancing together and felt the magic again, not just the buzz, the magic.

*"And then she looks at me
The darkness disappears, I long to be
That special someone that she hopes to see,
And I pray she'll free the other side....
I know if she were mine,
Forever in my heart a light will shine
To show the way, tomorrow we'd define
As she opens up the other side....of me."*

With this line Cinders drifted off stage leaving the Prince to ponder a possible future without his newly found love.

Freddie was starting to relax and enjoy this.

*"But how do I tell her
And just what should I say?
She may not feel the same as I do
Then she'll think that I'm foolish,
It might push her away
Then my pitiful life would be through....
But then she smiles my way
With eyes so full of love that I must stay
To be with her for more than just this day
I just have to be the other side....of me."*

The mood and tempo of the music changed and Freddie stepped away from the microphone and out of the booth. The Prince and the dancers continued to act out a dramatic sequence designed to give Cinders time to get into her glad rags and board the crystal coach.

Lisa was in floods of happy tears.

"Wow I'm really surprised how much I'm enjoying this," he chirped. "But how does it sound?"

"You must be joking if you think I can even speak," she sobbed.

"But is it okay?" he asked.

She nodded wildly and hugged him.

She dried her eyes and they held hands, captivated by the music as it continued, something they had done so often, on a different stage in a different world many years ago.

"Do you miss this Freddie?" she asked.

"Not really," he said, "We've written a much better script together and who knows what would have happened to us but for..."

Now it was his turn to bite his lip.

"Everything for a reason."

"Freddie," Scotty called over in a loud whisper and gestured at the booth. Cinderella was ready to make her grand entrance stage right. It was time to finish the act.

Freddie stepped back up to the microphone but this time kept hold of his lovely Lisa's hand.

> *"And when you look at me*
> *I hope you'll see the one you'll love, and we*
> *Will always be together, endlessly*
> *And there can be another side....*
> *Please say you'll be right here*
> *To hold my hand and chase away this fear*
> *My every dream becoming crystal clear*

As you open up the other side...."
"I know that there's another side....
Please God she frees the other side....of me."

The lights dimmed, the music faded and the house tabs closed. The audience erupted into a barrage of appreciative applause. Freddie quietly reflected, a million happy thoughts racing through his already overcrowded mind.

He could even imagine his little worry monkey in anguish as several demons were finally put to rest and dismissed completely.

A crowd of excited cast members were gathering in the wings, bombarding Roy and Sanjay with questions.

Freddie didn't want a fuss, so remained hidden from view in the booth.

"Can you go and ask Scotty to clear the stage please," he asked Lisa quietly. "I'm going to need a little time to myself."

Lisa smiled and scurried off.

Scotty did an excellent job of moving people along.

"Please folks we need to set for the second act, you should quickly make your way to the dressing rooms please."

Once everyone had gone Freddie left the booth and went over to Roy and Sanjay who were waiting patiently to thank him.

Sanjay slapped his back while his uncle gave him a huge bear hug.

"I still find all this contact from you a little hard to get used to Roy."

"I'm just grateful I have such a wonderful and

talented nephew. Well done Freddie I always knew you still had it in you."

"And you'll get someone else as soon as possible?"

"No way, the jobs yours."

"But I don't want it."

"Well I'll look."

He took an exaggerated glance over both shoulders. "Too bad there's no one available."

"Tell you what then I'll ask Steve to do it."

Roy looked horrified.

"Hang on a minute," he said, "You told me earlier that you'd never damage my reputation."

"Just look Roy, that's all I ask, look hard."

Scotty came over to join the group.

"Thanks for all your help lad," Freddie said. "Are we all set ready for act two?"

"Is that it Boss?" Scotty said, quiet obviously stunned by the event.

"Is what it?"

"You steal the show, shock every single one of us into the middle of next week and all you want to know is are we ready for act two?"

"Okay then, did you enjoy your first unsupervised run on the book?"

"It's been different."

"Great, well I think you're doing a superb job lad, keep it up."

Oscar came bustling towards them with a large glass of something familiar.

"Here Freddie my darling boy drink this, you deserve it. What a voice."

"Thanks, am I allowed this?"

"It's okay Boss," Scotty said. "Under the

circumstances I'll turn a blind eye this time."

"You cheeky little shit, I was asking my wife."

"Of course sweetie," Lisa said, "I'll turn a blind eye this time as well."

"Erm, Boss," Scotty said with a big grin.

"What lad?"

"Watch your language on my stage."

Everybody chuckled except Freddie.

"In that case lad 'bollocks, bollocks, bollocks'."

Scotty looked worried.

"Now...ban me. Please, I'm begging you."

Twenty

Tuesday 24th Christmas Eve - Freddie had valiantly fought to put the Christmas tree up in the morning.

The massive artificial spruce, which totally filled the large bay window in the living room, had been in the family since his childhood.

The decorating of the tree was something he and Lisa had always done together since the year they married and moved into the house he'd inherited from his parents.

It was an activity that brought back some very special memories for them both and they'd created a few more of their own along the way.

More recently the tree and some of the baubles were showing some considerable signs of ageing and although Lisa wouldn't normally tolerate anything tatty in her beautiful home, these precious items would always be allowed to remain.

This year she'd added some beautiful Medina glass baubles and then finished it off with thick luxuriant gold and red tinsel and tartan ribbon bows.

By midday the living room was awash with twinkling lights, festive ornaments and a simple nativity montage sat on the mantle over the fire surrounded by a few personal greetings cards.

Around one o'clock in the afternoon Oscar, Roy and Claire had arrived and proceeded to smuggle bags full of delightfully wrapped surprises from the car and up into their rooms.

Drinks were served and everyone started to relax a little with a light lunch of sandwiches and nibbles.

The laying of the dining table was next on the agenda.

Table cloths, runners and place mats were neatly laid and then it was furnished with all of the trappings ready for the special festive feast.

Lisa had emerged from the kitchen long enough to supervise, making sure everything was being put in exactly the right place.

Glasses and cutlery were polished and the red and gold theme continued, including candy twist candles, very expensive looking crackers and sprinkled glitter everywhere. The completed table looked fit to grace the front cover of any high end magazine.

Delighted with their highly creative handy work Oscar had demanded that Freddie hurry up and put the finishing touches to the mulled wine as a well deserved reward for all of them.

And all the time they'd chatted and laughed.

Freddie had specifically noticed that his lovely Lisa was looking particularly contented and didn't appear to be anywhere near as stressed about the whole occasion as in previous years.

"Are you happy?" he'd asked, passing her a small

glass of the warm spicy wine.

She leant her head on his shoulder and smiled.

"Very," she'd replied.

The two girls had then spent the rest of the afternoon preparing things in the kitchen, whilst the boys watched a movie on the telly and generally stayed out of the way.

It had been a cold day but fortunately remained dry, so at around seven o'clock they'd all wrapped up warm and headed off for a stroll around the lake in the park to clear their heads and blow away the cobwebs.

The park was full of people enjoying the festive displays, the trees all covered in white twinkling lights entwined around the leafless branches, which reflected off the rippling water of the lake to produce a mesmerising effect.

A perfectly enchanting place to wander through.

They'd slowly made their way to the late carol service at the parish church.

This wasn't a favourite activity for the boys but they always agreed to go for the benefit of the lovely Lisa, who also happened to be the one who would be feeding them well over the next couple of days, so they considered it was a fair exchange.

Now they were safely back home in the warm, and busily tucking into hot roast beef and horseradish sandwiches on thickly cut homemade bread, still warm from the bread maker.

Lisa had left them both cooking when they'd gone out for the walk, and as Freddie had opened the front door on their return they'd been greeted with the most incredible aroma.

"Well lad this has been a grand day."

Roy said with a grin. "For me this is the start of a very special Christmas and it feels just perfect."

He took a huge bite out of his sandwich.

"And who would have thought you'd have something special to be grateful for this year Uncle."

"Indeed I have," he said. "Cinderella is going to make me a tidy profit this year and..."

He couldn't continue the joke as Claire's face was a picture of disappointment.

"I'm pulling your leg my dear," he laughed.

He placed his hand on her knee.

"You are undoubtedly the best thing that has happened to me in a very long while."

"Really? Oh that's so sweet of you to say so."

"I mean I was really struggling to find a fairy."

"You cheeky bugger Royston Hobbs."

She playfully slapped his had away.

"And there was me thinking you were after my body."

"I am, preferably in a sparkly tutu and tights."

"Oh please stop it you two!!" Freddie called out

"Why do I always have to end up with a head full of indecent images."

"It's payback for the cynical suggestion that we wouldn't last." Roy laughed.

"It sounds like you had absolutely no hope for him in the romance department Freddie," said Claire.

"I didn't if I'm honest, I could never see anyone putting up with his obsessive habits. But as I said before, I'm more than happy to be proved wrong."

"But I don't have to put up with any of his 'obsessive habits' as you put it, he hasn't got any."

"At least none that you've seen yet," Oscar added with a laugh.

"He's a lot different these days Claire, you just need to pray he doesn't revert to Old Roy."

"I am here you know."

"What's he going to turn into then, something hideous and cruel? I really worry when you say things like this?"

"Ah it's worry monkey time," said Freddie.

"Now look what you've started," said Roy.

"Shut up Freddie. No one wants to hear about your bizarre monkey fetish tonight."

He turned to Claire with a smile.

"Now I admit that maybe, just maybe over the years I've been a little bit dull and predictable."

"Maybe?" asked Freddie.

"A little bit predictable?" added Lisa.

"Okay, I was very predictable," Roy admitted.

"But you were never dull Uncle," Freddie added.

"I really liked the Old Roy, he was a gentleman and a sweetheart. But I prefer the improved version."

"Thank you Oscar."

"You're welcome Roy."

They chinked glasses.

"Joking aside." Roy turned back to Claire again.

"I really am glad Freddie asked me to come along that Tuesday evening to watch you perform. It was a very welcome 'me' changing moment."

"For me too, and it all happened exactly four weeks ago tonight."

"Only four weeks?" Lisa asked, "Seems much longer."

"I just wish I'd met this sexy man much sooner."

Claire smiled sweetly as she leant over and gently kissed him.

"Please stop that," Freddie implored.

"Inappropriate images are just flooding back into my head again."

"Shut up Freddie," said Roy "And go play with your monkey because we're very happy and I'm going to keep doing this just to annoy you."

He kissed Claire again.

"And I would like to thank the rest of you for your good wishes last week when you toasted us, it obviously worked as we've had a very successful opening."

"Then I think that deserves another toast."

"Not again Freddie," said Oscar.

"Why not?"

"We did all this last time."

"We do it every time."

"Okay fair enough, what to then?"

"Roy and Claire the Fairy."

"This better not be going where it went last time my dear boy."

"Where did it go? Oh yes I remember we toasted my sperm."

"That and a few other things," Oscar laughed.

Freddie noticed that Lisa had gone quite and was deep in thought.

"What day is it?" she demanded suddenly.

"Christmas Eve silly."

"No I meant what day is it?"

"Tuesday," everyone said at once.

"Oh my God," Lisa exclaimed.

"What's the matter?"

"In all the fuss of the last couple of days I'd forgotten."

"Forgotten what?"

"I'm late."

"What for?" asked Roy.

"How long?" Claire said excitedly. She sat forward on the sofa with a huge smile.

"Two days. But I'm never late. Always twenty six days, never more never less."

Tears started to well up in her eyes.

Roy looked really confused. "Can someone tell please me what's going on?"

Oscar stood up in a daze, there appeared to be tears in his eyes as well. He walked to the sideboard and picked up the bottle of scotch.

"Oscar?" Roy asked.

"Anyone for a top up?"

"Freddie! I'm late."

"It's only two days sweetie, don't get yourself all worked up, let wait and see."

"But you must understand. I've never ever been late."

Twenty One

Wednesday 25th Christmas Day - Freddie woke to find he was alone, but the room was filled with the most wonderful aroma of zesty spices and roasting meat.

He sat up and once he was comfily propped up by a mound of pillows he allowed himself to drift into the spirit of the occasion.

He loved Christmas.

As a child his parents had always made a big fuss about it being a special time for family, but in some ways Freddie never really understood why.

There had only ever been just the three of them and his Uncle Roy, who'd spent most weekends taking them out for a drive in his old Bentley.

They'd walk through the countryside, lunch at a country pub and occasionally take a trip to the theatre on a Saturday night where Freddie had gained his love for the performing arts.

Every weekend had been a special time for the family, and Christmas had seemed like any other weekend.

Except for the presents.

Excitement would usually wake him early and in the dark he'd work his way eagerly to a pillowcase full of small gifts at the bottom of his bed. As he tore off the wrapping he would always close his eyes and allow the glorious smell of roasting turkey to fill his memory, just as it was doing right now.

His memory was suddenly flooded with happy laughter, of hugs and tears, celebrations and congratulations.

Had it all been a dream?

Was he still dreaming?

Then he heard her singing.

He must be awake because in his dreams the lovely Lisa always had a sweet singing voice. The tuneless noise he now heard coming up the stairs could only mean one thing.

Everything was going to be just perfect.

Twenty Two

January 2014

Wednesday 8th 3.25 am - Freddie was back in a very familiar place.

He looked around the irregular drab space then walking across the brightly coloured carpet towards a rather narrow white door with a well worn brass knob, he knocked on the door.

"Are you in there monkey?"

"You know I am." came the muffled reply. "It's impossible to avoid me forever Freddie and I knew you'd be back sooner rather than later."

Freddie reached out to grab the cold tarnished door knob and despite a growing feeling of anguish he pulled on it hard. The door creaked as it opened and Freddie peered into the dark void beyond.

"Come on out monkey, I want to see you for what you are."

Two bright eyes suddenly appeared from the shadows and as they moved closer the features of a cute little creature came into view.

As it reached the doorway it stepped half a pace into Freddie's room.

"There you are monkey and that's close enough. But your innocent looks deceive."

"I am what you see Freddie, I exist because you let me."

"Oh I know I'll never be rid, but I'm getting better at controlling you because I see through your disguise. And I know that what happens in my life is down to me. Good or bad I can say with certainty you can't change anything."

"Unless of course you let me."

"You've over estimated your influence monkey, I no longer fear you."

"Give it time, there is always something on the horizon. You can't yet imagine the extra worry you're about to encounter, and the more you gather around you to love, the more you'll see of me."

It hopped from one leg to the other whooping in apparent glee.

"Right now monkey there's only one thing that's worrying me."

"What did I tell you, there's always a worry."

"It's time to move on, time to enjoy what we're given and stop worrying about what may or may not happen."

"You said you had a worry, tell me what it is."

Freddie placed his hand on the edge of the door and his knuckles whitened.

Looking firmly into the creatures eyes he raised an eyebrow, then with one swift movement he slammed the door shut.

Monkey shrieked in pain as it hit him fully in the

face, propelling him back into the darkness of the room.

"I was worried that I might feel terribly guilty about doing that."

Freddie brushed his hands together as a broad grin spread across his face.

"But strangely I don't, so no worries out here at all now monkey."

There was a groan from the other side of the door.

"Freddie."

"What?"

"That was cruel and it really hurt."

"Good."

"Was it really necessary?"

"Everything for a reason monkey, and a reason for everything."

ACKNOWLEDGEMENTS

Jamie Gray would like to thank all his family and friends for putting up with his incessant wittering and fussing about this novel and their kind words of encouragement during the three years of its creation. Mainly he would like to thank his eldest brother Steve for introducing him to the world of musical theatre all those years ago, and his mate Simon for the many wonderful fishing trips they've shared in a forlorn attempt to keep his sanity intact. He'd also like to mention SOLAR Services and all the societies he's ever had the privilege to work with and he's grateful for all the happy memories they've shared together.

www.jamiegrayauthor.wordpress.com
Twitter: @jamiegrayauthor
Email: jamiegrayauthor@hotmail.com

Printed in Poland
by Amazon Fulfillment
Poland Sp. z o.o., Wrocław